Everything you —*and more*— *about*

WORLD'S MOST ELIGIBLE BACHELOR
Duncan MacNeill

Occupation: "I'm a DEA agent—not a daddy! Though my recent experience delivering a baby boy to a mysterious and beautiful woman has certainly given *her* ideas."

Any Secrets? "I wouldn't call it a secret, but I *am* heir to my family's fortune. Not that my being a millionaire makes a difference. When it comes to catching criminals and protecting women and children, I get down in the trenches just like anyone else."

Favorite Pastimes: "These days—with a pretty amnesiac and her newborn baby in my life— seems all I've been doing is diapering the baby and warming bottles. Not my usual thing, but it does have its moments."

Marriage Vow: "I didn't think I even had a heart behind my steel badge. But this lovely new mom and her bundle of joy might just melt my icy heart."

Dear Reader,

Thank you for joining us for another WORLD'S MOST ELIGIBLE BACHELORS book. This brand-new series has some of the finest authors in romance writing the stories of twelve unforgettable heroes.

Every month we'll follow the story of an utterly sexy, overwhelmingly desirable male who's been named a World's Most Eligible Bachelor by fictitious *Prominence Magazine*. We'll also bring you all the delectable details about each romance that has these confirmed bachelors changing their marital status to "taken"!

This month, RITA Award-winning author Marie Ferrarella's bachelor is Duncan MacNeill, a sexy and mysterious DEA agent. Duncan has a serious love of danger coursing through his veins. But does he have room in his heart for a precious newborn and the baby's amnesiac mommy? This brand-new story is also part of the author's bestselling THE BABY OF THE MONTH CLUB series.

And be sure to join us next month, when bestselling author Dixie Browning continues her series THE LAWLESS HEIRS. *His Business, Her Baby* is the story of a powerful executive forced into some much-needed rest and relaxation with a gorgeous—and very pregnant—heroine.

Until next time...here's to romance wishes and bachelor kisses!

The Editors

Please address questions and book requests to:
Silhouette Reader Service
U.S.: 3010 Walden Ave., P.O. Box 1325, Buffalo, NY 14269
Canadian: P.O. Box 609, Fort Erie, Ont. L2A 5X3

World's Most Eligible Bachelors

Marie Ferrarella

Detective Dad

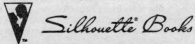

Silhouette Books

Published by Silhouette Books

America's Publisher of Contemporary Romance

To
Ann Leslie Tuttle,
and new friendships

 SILHOUETTE BOOKS

ISBN 0-373-65019-1

DETECTIVE DAD

Copyright © 1998 by Marie Rydzynski-Ferrarella

All rights reserved. Except for use in any review, the reproduction
or utilization of this work in whole or in part in any form by any
electronic, mechanical or other means, now known or hereafter
invented, including xerography, photocopying and recording, or in
any information storage or retrieval system, is forbidden without
the written permission of the editorial office, Silhouette Books,
300 East 42nd Street, New York, NY 10017 U.S.A.

All characters in this book have no existence outside the imagination of
the author and have no relation whatsoever to anyone bearing the same
name or names. They are not even distantly inspired by any individual
known or unknown to the author, and all incidents are pure invention.

This edition published by arrangement with Harlequin Books S.A.

® and TM are trademarks of Harlequin Books S.A., used under license.
Trademarks indicated with ® are registered in the United States Patent
and Trademark Office, the Canadian Trade Marks Office and in other
countries.

Printed in U.S.A.

A Conversation with...
RITA Award-winning author
MARIE FERRARELLA

What hero have you created for WORLD'S MOST ELIGIBLE BACHELORS, and how has he earned the coveted title?

MF: My hero would probably fit into the strong, silent—although not too silent—type. He earned the role because, besides being well-to-do, my hero was the center of a highly publicized DEA drug bust.

This original title is part of THE BABY OF THE MONTH CLUB, a Silhouette cross-line miniseries. What about this series so appeals to you? Do you have spinoffs planned?

MF: I have always loved miniseries and sagas, the chance to become involved with first one member of a family (or group), then another. We don't go through life alone, and neither should our heroes and heroines. The doctor whom the hero in this story turns to is the same doctor who delivered the other babies, as well as having her own story. I have two single titles in the offing that are directly tied to this baby club: *In the Family Way,* available June 1998, plus another title, *Baby Talk,* that will be published in September 1999.

What modern-day personality best epitomizes a WORLD'S MOST ELIGIBLE BACHELOR?

MF: Until he hooked up with his lady love, Pierce Brosnan was an A-1 World's Most Eligible Bachelor. Suave, handsome, with a sense of humor and a confidence that isn't overbearing, he is my idea of the perfect hero. (Okay, so I was swayed by Remington Steele and James Bond, but hey, what are dreams for?)

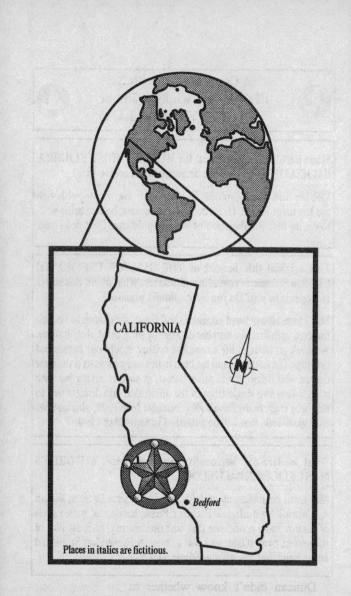

CALIFORNIA

N

• Bedford

Places in italics are fictitious.

One

Fog descended around him with the suddenness of a gasp. It surrounded him, not like a virginal white veil but like an ermine wrap, thick, heavy and completely impenetrable. Visibility went from nominal on the dark road to nonexistent.

Just what he needed.

Duncan MacNeill bit off a curse. He was in a hurry to get home, in a hurry to put the day and its annoying details far behind him.

This fog wasn't helping his mood any.

Neither was the article in the magazine that sat next to him on the seat of his Mercedes. The magazine was courtesy of Tony Fontana, another agent at the DEA. Fontana was as close to a friend as Duncan would allow himself at the agency. At least, he'd thought of Fontana as a friend up until now. But after Fontana had shown the magazine around, Duncan wasn't so sure. Everybody who'd seen it thought it was a hoot, except him.

The article that was such a sore point was courtesy of *Prominence Magazine,* which had selected him as this month's World's Most Eligible Bachelor, a title Duncan was certain the editors had dreamed up purely to raise sales.

Duncan didn't know whether to be insulted or

amused. There was a case for both, so he settled for
just being annoyed.

He gripped the steering wheel as he slowed his
pace, but not his impatience. Lately everything
seemed annoying to him. It was undoubtedly because
he felt restless again. The undercover job was over
and he'd been called back out of circulation. Politely
put, he'd been placed at a desk and taken off field
duty for his own safety until things blew over. Right
now, it didn't seem as if they ever would.

He was faced with marking time, helping to sort
things out as the Justice Department prepared to take
on the defendants of the Bogotá drug cartel, defendants he'd been instrumental in arresting. But all that
was in the past, and he was here, in the present, waiting things out.

He wasn't any good at waiting.

Duncan supposed that could be traced to his background. Instant gratification—that had been the credo
indelibly imprinted on his family's crest. The only
child of Stewart and Amanda MacNeill was to have
everything he wanted, when he wanted it.

Everything but the two things he'd desired. Their
time and their love. Neither had even remotely entered the picture.

Duncan scrubbed a hand over his face as he wove
his way up the hill toward his house. Why was he
letting himself get so maudlin tonight?

Maybe it had something to do with the fact that
his birthday was less than a month away. Thirty-two.
Somehow, he'd thought he would be somewhere else
in his life when he reached that age. It wasn't security he craved. He had more than enough of that.
And it wasn't even excitement, although that was

part of what made him turn his back on the family business and go into law enforcement. He wanted to make a difference. Anonymously. After spending the first half of his life being photographed and hounded as the heir apparent of one of the country's richest families, he'd discovered the immense appeal of undercover work. He found he really liked anonymity.

But being the center of quite possibly the biggest South American drug bust of the decade had squelched that. If he'd had any doubts, there was the dubious honor of World's Most Eligible Bachelor to remind him that he was back in the limelight.

Which brought him back to his current melancholy. All the money he could ever want and a career he enjoyed still couldn't snuff out the restlessness that periodically descended on him out of nowhere and threatened to dissolve any peace of mind he might have earned.

Duncan sighed. He wished now that he'd had that drink with Fontana. It might have dulled the edge on what he was feeling. But probably not. He wasn't much for drinking, anyway, and this wasn't the kind of night you wanted to have dulled senses.

He blinked as two tiny red embers emerged in the road up ahead.

What the—

Beams. They were beams, not embers. Two beams of light, cutting through the thick curtain of fog like the gleaming red eyes of some mythical creature in a long-forgotten fable.

The image barely had time to register before Duncan realized that he was driving straight into the back of a stalled car.

Swearing, he slammed on the brakes and turned

the steering wheel sharply to the left to avoid slamming into the car, then to the right, fighting to regain control of his vehicle. The Mercedes swerved from side to side on the road like a skid row drunk several drinks past his limit.

The impact rattled Duncan's teeth as the front right bumper of his car clipped the left rear of the stalled vehicle. The contact didn't seem to slow him down any as his car continued to slide wildly. Tires squealed as he skidded. An eternity later, it was over. The Mercedes came to a shaken halt, having completely turned around, and the left side of his car was up higher than the right.

Had he butted up against the hill?

For a minute, turned inside out, Duncan couldn't tell. His brain tried to piece together the terrain he'd covered. The road from the federal building he'd left half an hour ago to the stone house on top of Spy Glass Hill, the house his parents had left him, was long and winding. With the fog obscuring any sort of view, he could be anywhere along that path. There were no markers for him to go by. All he was certain of was that the other driver had to be crazy to have stopped dead like that, without any warning. His hazard lights weren't even flashing. What the hell was wrong with him?

Shaken, angry, Duncan stormed out of his car. He left the door hanging open as he looked around for the other vehicle.

It had been shoved off the road by the impact of the collision.

Perilously close, he realized as he approached it, to the edge of the embankment.

If he had seen it just a moment later, or hit it any

harder than he had, he would have sent the car and its occupants plummeting over the side, more than likely to their death.

Adrenaline pumped through him, ignited by the near miss. "What the hell do you think you're doing?" he shouted at the driver before he even reached the car. "I could have killed you!"

The very thought left him in a cold sweat. He could have been found guilty of manslaughter through no fault of his own. The thought that he had possibly come within inches of killing an innocent person was unbearable. It was hard enough facing that possibility every day in his line of work when it might mean saving his own life. To be confronted with it out of the blue like this set him on edge.

The car, a blue '92 Mazda, looked battered and worn before its time. The mark of a careless driver. But he already knew that.

Duncan struggled to contain his rage. Yanking the car door open, he was ready to haul the driver out and give him a piece of his mind.

Anger disappeared into the fog the moment he looked inside.

There was only one occupant in the car. A dazed, pale young woman. Her blond hair was damp, plastered to her face as if the fog had found a way to seep in through the sealed windows. There was a single, thin stream of blood oozing its way down the side of her cheek from a fresh cut at her temple. Pain was etched along her face.

Looking at her, Duncan had no idea how she had even managed to get behind the wheel of her car. There was absolutely no room for her to maneuver.

Hugely pregnant, she would have been ripe enough to burst if she'd been a melon.

A fresh battalion of feelings marched through him, stomping down his impatience and unearthing concern instead.

"Oh my God, are you all right?"

Was she all right? The words played through her brain in slow motion. They didn't evoke an answer. Not even a silent one.

She didn't know.

She looked at him, dazed, speechless. Robbed of any thoughts. Robbed of everything but the pain that was searing through her loins, threatening to rip her in two at any moment.

Rather than answer, she clutched at his hand when he offered it, squeezing it. Squeezing it hard, as if that could somehow transfer some of the pain she was feeling to him, to somewhere else. At least for a little while, until she caught her breath.

It didn't work.

She couldn't catch her breath. The pain, like the swell of her belly, refused to go away.

Duncan saw the drops of perspiration all along her brow. Some of it mingled with the blood at her temple. Guilt and embarrassment sliced through him. "Of course you're not all right. Any fool could see that." He realized he was staring at her stomach, but for the life of him, he couldn't draw his eyes away. "You look ready to explode." Helplessness threatened to overwhelm him. It wasn't a feeling he relished or was accustomed to. Or tolerated.

Gingerly, he touched the cut on her forehead. She closed her eyes, wincing. The way she clutched at her belly told him that she wasn't even aware of the cut, or his touch. Something of far greater proportion was happening.

Oh God, he hoped he was wrong. This was something his job didn't cover.

"Where am I?" she whispered. Her voice was reedy, distant.

He guessed that the bump on her head must have temporarily disoriented her.

"You were in an accident," he began. "My car—" The magnitude of what could have happened hit him again, leaving fresh marks. "Damn it, what were you thinking, stopped in the middle of the road like that?"

"I'm pregnant." It wasn't an answer to his question. It was a revelation to herself.

Pregnant.

How? When?

Who?

The words whispered along her fevered brain, teasing her. Mocking her. She tried to turn her head to look beside her. But there was no one sitting there. No one around but this stranger.

She was alone. The sensation vibrated through her, twining with the pain.

"Yes," Duncan agreed. "You're very pregnant." Why was she saying it as if it were a complete surprise to her? Did she have a concussion? Just how badly had she hit her head?

Duncan tried to think.

He leaned in closer to get a better look at the gash at her temple. The woman stiffened, drawing in her breath. Her eyes widened as she looked up at him, frightened. For a second, Duncan thought she was afraid of him, then realized that he had nothing to do with the look in her eyes.

"The baby—I'm—"

She didn't finish. She didn't have to. Duncan knew, even as he asked her, "Are you trying to tell me you're going into labor?"

The woman made no response.

They needed help. Duncan fumbled with his free hand for the cell phone in his pocket. "I need my hand," he told her, attempting to gently pull it free.

She didn't seem to hear him. And she didn't let go. She held on, held on so tightly that the circulation felt as if it were leaving his fingers. It was almost as if she thought that if she let go, she would tumble over the edge and be swallowed up by the pain.

"Fine. Okay," Duncan agreed gamely. "I can do this with one hand."

Leaving his one hand within her death grip, he pulled out his phone with the other. Duncan drew the antenna out with his teeth, extending it to its limit. Angling the small phone into a better position, he hit 911 with his thumb, then pressed Send.

A whiny, staccato noise was emitted almost immediately. It sounded like the heartbeat of a tired amateur runner. His call hadn't registered.

It figured.

Exasperated, he tried again with the same results. The third time, he flipped the phone shut.

The signal wasn't getting through.

Perfect.

Duncan shoved the phone back into his pocket. The woman's breathing had turned into panting. He was wasting time standing here.

"I can't get anyone," he told her needlessly. Duncan looked around, frustrated. He still couldn't see anything. For now, they were cut off from the rest of the world. "The fog must be interfering with the signal. Listen, do you think you can hang on?" He wrapped his other hand around hers. The added pressure was meant to be encouraging, but he doubted she even felt it. "I can drive you to hospital."

She shook her head vehemently at the suggestion, her eyes widening as pain seared through her again, fresh, sharp and all-consuming.

Maybe she was just panicking, Duncan hoped. In her condition, it was perfectly understandable. "When did you start—"

"I don't know," she gasped. There was no point in letting him finish. She had no answer for any of his questions. No answer for any of hers.

She was still disoriented, he thought. Under the circumstances, he couldn't blame her. Where the hell was her husband or significant other? he wondered angrily. Or whoever it was who had gotten her into this condition in the first place. Didn't this woman have any family? And what the hell was she doing, driving alone on a night like this?

Damn it, didn't she have any common sense at all?

Or maybe, he relented, gaining control over his nerves, she didn't have any choice in the matter. That could be it.

"Were you on your way to the hospital?" he asked her kindly.

Why was he asking her so many questions? And why didn't she have the answer to any of them? she wondered anxiously.

Why didn't she know? Why was there nothing for

her to draw on when she tried to think? To remember?

But there wasn't anything. Just a huge emptiness looming all around her.

"I don't know," she repeated. "I don't know."

The words sounded almost frantic to Duncan, like the last gasps of someone who was drowning and trying desperately to stay alive just one more second.

Compassion rose and elbowed the questions aside. This wasn't the time to badger her. He'd satisfy his curiosity later, after this ordeal was over and he had her somewhere other than on a fog-shrouded hill.

He realized they were pressing their luck, staying here like this. Any vehicle coming up the hill could hit them, just as he had hit her. Duncan thought of the flares in his trunk.

"It's all right." His voice was soft, soothing. "You don't need to answer me right now. It's going to be all right," Duncan promised. He tried not to dwell on the fact that he hadn't a clue as to how he was going to make good on his promise. "I'll be right back."

"Back? Back from where?" The breathless question was underlined in panic.

"I'm just getting some flares out of my trunk." His voice was already distant.

Was he leaving her? He couldn't.... She tried to call to him, but nothing came out.

And then she thought she heard footsteps. Drawing closer. He was back. He hadn't deserted her.

Exhausted, she let out a breath slowly, trying to find enough energy to speak before the next salvo of pain found her.

But it came all too quickly, following directly on

the heels of the other. Her hands flayed around until she came in contact with something. With him. Without meaning to, she dug her nails into his flesh.

"It's happening," she cried, arching against the unyielding bucket seat. "It's happening!"

Duncan had set the flares out on the road as quickly as possible and returned to her—just in time to encounter another death grip. He worked to loosen her fingers just a little, but he could feel each one of her nails as they sank in.

"That much I figured out on my own. All right, I'm going to move you into the back seat and drive you—"

"No—no time." She snapped out the words as she twisted and writhed, trying to outdistance the pain. Like a heat-seeking missile, it found her at every turn.

Helplessness swelled within Duncan. He knew how to talk his way out of a tight situation, how to negotiate and face down an adversary. None of that meant anything now. "I was afraid you were going to say that."

He knew nothing about this part of the life cycle other than the fact that it happened all the time, every day. To other people. But he didn't have so much as a nature film to fall back on. The prospect of helping a woman bring a baby into the world unnerved him the way nothing else ever had.

She had to hold on until he could get some help for her. He wasn't the one to help her through this. Still holding her hand, he tried to appeal to her logically. This wasn't the way a new life was supposed to begin, on a fog-enshrouded, isolated road. Surely she could wait a little longer. After all, this was her baby they were talking about.

"Look," he began, wishing he had more words at his disposal, but his brain seemed to be numbed, "I've never done this before."

She wanted to laugh, to cry. Most of all, she wanted to hold on to something, to someone. Trying to rise above the pain, she looked at this man who was trying so hard to divorce himself from what was happening.

"I don't think I have, either."

She didn't *think* she'd gone through this before? The words struck Duncan. Didn't she know? Childbirth wasn't exactly something that floated whimsically out of your mind, like how many burritos you'd had the last time you ate at a Mexican restaurant, or whether or not you'd sustained a paper cut last week.

He looked at her eyes, wondering if she was on some sort of medication or, worse, doing drugs with a flagrant disregard for the life she was carrying. But the only thing he saw within the bright green depths was fear. Fear she was struggling to contain before it got the better of her. He knew the signs.

It was the fear that spoke to him. That aroused something within him that Duncan wasn't quite sure what to make of. For lack of a better term, he supposed it could be called a sense of charity. With it came duty.

There was no way around it. It was up to him. And her. The fog, by simultaneously bringing them together and then isolating them, had made them partners. So he would make the best of a bad situation. The way he'd been trained to do.

"All right, I'm always open to new experiences."

He smiled at the woman, trying to sound encouraging. "How about you?"

It was a moment before she could answer. A moment before the pain *let* her answer. "I don't think I have a choice." It felt as if this baby that she couldn't remember conceiving and had no memory of carrying, wanted to erupt into the world immediately. There was no holding it back any longer.

I wish you did, Duncan thought, though he kept it to himself. "Doesn't look that way," he agreed out loud.

Collecting himself, he tried to approach the situation logically. The first thing he needed was light so he could see what he was doing, although the thought didn't hearten him.

"All right, if we're going to do this, I really am going to need both my hands—" It suddenly occurred to him that he was about to share life's greatest miracle with her and he still had no idea who she was. "What's your name?"

Rather than answer, the woman paused, as if she didn't trust him enough to tell him. Or, and this was so ludicrous that he discarded the thought immediately, she didn't know.

It took her a minute. And then, from out of the abyss, came something familiar. A name. Her name.

"Madison," she finally said.

"Madison," he repeated, nodding. It was unusual, but for some reason, it seemed to fit her. "I'm Duncan and I need my hand."

As soon as she loosened her grip, he turned to walk away from her. She didn't have the strength to follow or even to make a grab for him. Was he leaving her, after all?

"Where are you going?" Had she said that before? Muddled, frightened, she wasn't sure. She wasn't sure of anything.

The panic Duncan heard almost had him turning back to comfort her. But a sense of urgency had taken over. Something told him that time was short. He answered without turning around. "Just to get my car."

She didn't understand. She'd already told him there was no time to drive to the hospital. No time to do anything except surrender to the pain. She didn't want to face it alone. "Why?"

It sounded so faint, Duncan wasn't sure if he imagined the question. He answered anyway, raising his voice so she could hear him as he climbed into the car.

"I want to turn it around and aim the headlights in this direction so I can see better. You're laboring under enough of a handicap as it is, no pun intended."

"None...taken." She barely gasped the words out, clawing at the cushion beneath her.

She'd never felt such pain before. At least, she didn't think she had. But there was no before, not for her. For her, there was nothing except now. Her life, the only life she knew, had begun five minutes ago, when she'd opened her eyes and looked up into the face of an angry stranger.

Pain, hot and throbbing, surrounded her in a slick, cylindrical tube, giving her nowhere to go, nowhere to hide. The only salvation lay in clawing her way up to the light that was coming to her from the top of the cylinder. Shining at her.

Guiding her.

Headlights, she realized. The light she saw coming at her belonged to the headlights of a car. The stranger's car. No, not a stranger, Duncan. Duncan's car. He'd turned it around, just as he'd said. He hadn't left her. A sliver of relief created a place for itself amid the pain that drenched her.

Madison struggled not to faint. Her mind, what there was of it, winked in and out like a firefly flirting with the night.

And then he was beside her. She felt his presence, sensed it. Tears formed at the corners of her eyes. Or was that perspiration? She couldn't tell.

"You didn't leave," she murmured.

He'd been gone perhaps a minute, perhaps less. It had probably seemed like a lifetime to her. Duncan dug into his pocket and took out his handkerchief. Trying to be as gentle as possible, he dabbed at the gash at her temple. Blood soaked into the weave. Beneath it, the cut was smaller than he'd thought.

"What, and miss all this fun? Not on your life." Without thinking, he tossed the handkerchief aside. There was no room for her to lie down in the front. He had to move her. "Madison, if this is going to happen for us, I'm going to have to get you into the back seat."

The faintest glimmer of a smile crossed her dry lips as, just for a second, the pain receded. This poor man was trying his best, she thought. "I don't do that sort of thing on the first date."

Duncan laughed, surprised at her response. Some of the tension left him. At least she had a sense of humor, he thought. That helped a little.

"Looks like you've already had a first date, Madison." Duncan considered the logistics. He knew that it would be easier for him if he could pick her up, but it might be less stressful for her if she did this on her own. "Do you think you can stand up?"

At this point, it was all she could do to stay conscious. But she didn't want to admit it. Madison licked her lips, digging for strength. "I can try," she said weakly.

Turning, she dragged her legs out of the car. But as she started to rise from her seat, pain snapped its jaws shut around her.

The world disappeared as she felt her bones turn to pudding. The last thought that telegraphed across her mind was that she was falling. And that the world had suddenly lost its bottom.

Two

Startled, Duncan just managed to catch Madison before she hit the ground.

"Don't faint on me now, Madison!"

The hard jerk had her eyes flying open and seemed to bring her around again. Small wonder, Duncan thought. He could almost feel the jolt she'd gotten vibrating through his own body.

"That was close." He muttered the words more to himself than to her. She was far from stable on her feet. The thought of a repeat performance left him leery. "Here, maybe we should do this together."

With his arm around her back for support, Duncan helped Madison into the back seat of her car. Because of her condition and her unwieldy size, the maneuver was far from easy to execute, but moving gingerly, he finally managed to get her onto the seat and turned around into a reclining position.

Rounding the car quickly and getting in on the other side, Duncan couldn't help thinking that this put an entirely different spin on the meaning of tight spots for him.

The sharp intake of breath, three incomplete staccato sounds, dissolved his thoughts as he entered the car. It was evident that they were quickly running out of time. This was not good, he thought, not good at all. "Another one?"

Madison couldn't answer, couldn't trust herself to open her mouth without letting an ungodly sound escape. All she could do was press her lips together and struggle valiantly to hold back the screams that were throbbing urgently in her throat.

The outline of her lips disappeared into two ghostly white lines. Duncan had his answer.

"Another one," he murmured. They were coming much too fast for his liking.

It was really happening.

Hot, perspiring, Duncan stripped off his jacket and dropped it on the floor, then loosened his tie. With all his heart, he wished there was something he could do to postpone this ordeal, for both their sakes.

But wishing was a useless waste of time and he knew it. The lady was about to become a mother no matter what he wished and whether he helped or not. He hadn't chosen the path he was on in life just to remain on the sidelines when he was needed.

Duncan rolled up his sleeves.

He saw Madison's eyes widen and realized she was looking at his shoulder holster. It was so much a part of him, a part of who he was, he'd forgotten he was wearing it.

"It's okay," he assured her. "I'm supposed to be wearing one. I'm a cop."

It was a simpler explanation than telling her the truth. This wasn't the time to go into his career choice or the twists it had taken. Most people didn't even know what a DEA agent was. It wasn't like belonging to the FBI or even the CIA, letters everyone was familiar with.

His mind was wandering. Uneasiness did that to him sometimes. Duncan saw her eyes glaze over. His guess was that each contraction was following on the heels of the last.

"Looks like they're coming pretty fast and close."

Madison was barely aware of the half nod she gave. "Fast...close..."

The monosyllabic words were all she could manage. There was no air left in her lungs to form sentences. No energy left in her body that wasn't centered and trained on what was happening between her loins. She tried to clutch at something, but the vinyl beneath her wouldn't give and it eluded her fingertips.

The scratchy noise registered. Duncan was well acquainted with it. It was the sound of desperation. Show time, he thought.

He tried to remember what he needed to do besides offer paltry words of encouragement. It was too late for regrets, though for the first time he wished he had watched Ted Murphy's damn video when the man had offered to show it to him. Murphy's wife had given birth six months ago. For some reason unfathomable to Duncan, Murphy had faithfully recorded every gory second within the hospital, leading up to the baby's birth. On one of those rare occasions that Duncan had resurfaced in the DEA office, Murphy had tried to corner him for a private showing. At the time, Duncan had felt he had better things to do than see a video that was guaranteed to separate him from his last meal.

Now he wished he had watched.

But though he hadn't actually seen the video, Duncan hadn't been able to stop Murphy from talking about the event. Murphy had given him an abbreviated play-by-play and relentlessly gone on about the wondrous miracle he had been privileged to be a part of.

Miracle. Duncan remembered, inwardly sneering at the soppy sentiment. How much of a miracle was it when it had been going on since the beginning of time? His own mother had given birth to him and never considered it a miracle. Knowing her, she'd most likely viewed it as an uncomfortable inconvenience.

Duncan dug deep for Murphy's words now. He needed something to guide him. Anything to combat this helpless feeling he was experiencing. He didn't like not being in control of a situation, and this one was way out of his league.

Exhausted, Madison fell back against the hard seat. A puddle was pooling around her back. She was sticking to the upholstery and a damp, heavy scent assaulted her nose, offending it. Why was this happening to her? And how had she come to this point, this moment?

Why couldn't she remember anything?

The next moment, another contraction came, ripping aside her questions, her thoughts, and grabbing center stage for itself.

Duncan took a deep breath, bracing himself. He tried to get as comfortable as he could under the circumstances. Early Christian martyrs doing penance had had more elbow space than he had, he thought sarcastically.

He touched the hem of her dress, then hesitated. He'd seen brutality the average man didn't begin to dream of, yet invading someone's privacy when they had every right to it was offensive to him. Except for a twist of fate, this woman would have been in a hospital, being attended to by her own doctor, not lying in the back seat of her car with a stranger about to strip away all her clothing below her waist.

There was just no neat, tidy way to do this. He felt embarrassed for her as well as himself.

"I'm sorry, Madison, but I'm going to have to get very personal here."

Vinyl or not, she was on the verge of ripping through the upholstery with her nails. Madison strained to make out what he was saying. The haze around her was pulsating, threatening to separate her from the rest of the world again. She fought hard to hold on.

"I think…we've gotten…beyond…personal," she gasped.

Duncan pressed his lips together. "Right."

Clamping down on any feelings that weren't absolutely essential to the situation, Duncan gingerly pushed up Madison's dress. Then, as quickly, as impersonally as humanly possible, he stripped off her underwear. His eyes met hers briefly, a silent apology in them. She seemed to understand and nodded.

Or maybe she was just moving her head up and down, trying to fake out her pain and keep it from finding her for a moment.

It didn't matter.

What mattered was this baby, who was struggling so hard to fight its way into a world that was indifferent at best, harsh and cruel at worst.

Her heels digging into the seat, Madison arched her hips up as the pain clearly intensified to a dramatic degree. Afraid she'd fall off the seat, Duncan bracketed her body on that side with his arm, putting up a barrier to keep her in place.

"Steady," he ordered, the steely note in direct contrast to what he was feeling.

Perspiration beaded along his neck, sliding down his back in a crazy, zigzag free fall. The holster and the weapon it held dug into his ribs. He didn't have time to take it off. He didn't have any time left at all. It was happening.

"I think I—" Doubt vanished, replaced by an awed excitement that was completely foreign to him. "I see a head, Madison." Duncan widened his eyes as the magnitude of what was happening slammed into him with the force of a Mack truck hitting a brick wall. He looked at her, amazed as much at the miracle she was part of as at his own reaction to it. "I see the top of his head!"

More than once, he'd witnessed life ooze away from a man like so many grains of sand slipping into the bottom of an hourglass. Endings he understood. But a beginning, the start of a new life, well, this was something entirely different. Something he'd never been part of before.

Anticipation fine-tuned his nerves until they were taut, yet vibrating.

"His." Duncan had said "his." Madison strained to make a connection, to get her brain to focus on a coherent thought.

"It's a boy?" she gasped.

"I don't know." All he saw was the crown of the head. A dark crown. Her hair was blond. The thought came from nowhere and disappeared just as quickly. "I need more evidence." Duncan raised his eyes to her face. There were tears rolling down her cheeks, yet she wasn't crying. Tension? Pain? Probably both and more. "Madison, you have to push."

She'd already begun doing that on her own. Nothing on earth could have prevented her from pushing, not when all the forces of the world were bearing down on her this way.

"I am," she cried, too exhausted to be angry at the suggestion that she wasn't working as hard as she could to bring this baby into the world. "I am."

It wasn't enough. "Harder," Duncan commanded.

The order sounded dispassionate. A straggled, guttural moan escaped Madison's lips as she scrunched her eyes and concentrated every fiber of her being on expelling the tiny creature fighting for freedom within her.

Her color had turned to an alarming shade of red. Any moment, she was going to pass out. Duncan couldn't have that happening.

"Okay, stop, stop," he ordered, his voice rising. He heard himself panting along with her and made a conscious effort to control the response. "Take a deep breath."

Didn't he think she would if she could? Filling her lungs with air took second place only to getting rid of this devastating pain. "I...can't.... The baby... won't...let me."

If he accepted the excuse, he gave no sign. She couldn't allow this to get the better of her or she really would pass out.

"First thing you've got to learn is that you're in charge, not the baby."

He sounded like a drill sergeant, Madison thought bitterly.

How did she know that? Did she know any soldiers? Was her husband a soldier? She searched, but not a single answer emerged.

Again, the fact that she couldn't remember drove a sharp stiletto through the wall of pain, commanding her attention, if only for a second.

She didn't know if she had a husband.

"Now, take a deep breath," he instructed again, waiting. His eyes were on her and she tried, she really tried to do what he told her. But the air wouldn't come. Pain cut it off a second after she tried to pull it in.

She was in a bad way, Duncan thought. He wanted to try his phone again to see if he could raise someone, but there was no way he could turn his attention away from her even for a moment.

"Okay, let's try it again."

For the tiniest of seconds, the pain receded a fraction. Madison dug her elbows into the seat for leverage. The faintest of smiles whispered across her lips before they dissolved into pain-creased lines again.

"'Let's?'" she repeated. "Are...you delivering... too?"

"Sometimes I deliver," he answered dryly.

Yeah, he delivered. In his own way. Like in this last month. The only hitch was that the delivery had brought grave consequences with it. Exposing and destroying the Colombian-based drug cartel had managed to get his face plastered on the front page of every newspaper in the country, robbing him of the one thing he craved, the one thing money couldn't buy and he couldn't have. Anonymity.

Fear crept into Madison's heart again. He looked so serious. Was something wrong? Or was that just her imagination, striving to latch onto something? Her brain, so empty, so shaken, was drifting in and out, making little sense.

"You deliver...? I don't...understand."

He shook his head, dismissing his words. "Poor attempt at levity," he apologized, but he doubted she heard. Her face was contorted and turning an intense shade of red again. She was biting down on her lower lip so hard he was surprised it wasn't bleeding. "You know you can scream if you want," he urged.

He knew swearing sometimes helped to ease the tension that so regularly battered him. The same had to be true for rechanneling pain.

"All...I want...is...for this baby...to be...*born*." Madison twisted and writhed in the small space, bucking like a mustang encountering its first contact with a saddle.

"Okay, push." The stern order brooked no refusal. His eyes were on hers for moral support and to will her the energy she needed. "Push!"

"I *am*." The declaration ended in a piercing shriek as she bore down again.

They were almost there. Almost. But he still couldn't help her, still had no way to ease the child out. Impatience completely eradicated the last of his fear.

"Again!"

There was nothing left within her, not a shred of strength to draw on. She couldn't push anymore. Didn't he understand? How could he? Men didn't understand. Men just barked orders.

Angry, exhausted and teetering on the edge of hysteria, she tried to talk. "I—"

He knew that look he saw on her face. It was determination that was beginning to break up into smaller, splintered pieces. Dissolving. Once that happened, Duncan didn't know what would follow. He couldn't allow her to cave in now.

"Again!"

Damn him. Anger grew larger than the other emotions rampaging through her, bringing energy with it from some nebulous place. She tried once more. Bearing down. Straining.

Her lungs twisted from lack of air as every half breath escaped more quickly than it came. Knuckles white, eyes shut so tight they felt as if they were backing up into her very sockets, Madison pushed as if her life depended on it.

Or, at the very least, as if another, smaller life depended on it.

The air stilled within Duncan's chest as a tiny living being, naked, bloodied and shriveled, slid into his waiting hands. Duncan would have sworn his heart stopped in that instant.

The baby looked up at him. Huge, green, ageless eyes so like his mother's were staring into his. No sound, no wails, just a very intent, penetrating stare, as if somehow the seconds-old being knew who was holding him. It was absolutely, absurdly impossible, yet there it was. They knew each other.

Pulling back from the moment, Duncan looked around for something to clean the baby with. He had nothing but his jacket. He used it.

Why was Duncan being so quiet? Why wasn't the baby crying? What was wrong?

Madison vainly tried to push herself up into a semisitting position. The effort was doomed to failure.

"What—"

She was asking about the sex, Duncan thought, still unable to look away from the baby.

"A boy," he whispered. "It's a boy."

He was vaguely aware that his voice was hoarse and that it took effort to force out the words. The wonder of the moment was just beginning to penetrate his consciousness, taking over every corner like a slow-rising flood moving steadily upward until it covered everything in its path.

"You have a son."

With a great deal of effort, effort that surprised him, Duncan raised his eyes from the miracle he was holding in his arms to the sweat-drenched face of the woman he'd been so abruptly partnered with.

A miracle. He was holding a miracle. Damn if Ted Murphy hadn't been right after all.

"You have a son, Madison," Duncan repeated.

A son. She had a son. She had no last name, no recollection of anything more than a few minutes old, and she had a son.

Slowly, like a tired traveler in a foreign country, she tried to make sense of the words, the meaning of what she heard. She'd had no time to prepare for any of this, not her condition, not her situation or the suddenness of this tiny creature's arrival.

Yet even with this dearth, something overflowed within Madison's breast as she looked at the infant who had been, only moments before, part of her own body.

Very weakly, a smile curved the corners of her mouth. "A son," she murmured softly. Without knowing where the strength came from, she reached out with heavy arms to accept her son.

The cord, Duncan realized. He hadn't cut the umbilical cord yet. For a second, his mind was blank, and then he thought of the knife in his jacket pocket. It was a highly polished, pearl-handled Swiss knife. A token of esteem from Raul Montenegro, the one drug lord the DEA agents had failed to capture when the net had been pulled shut around the top men in the organization.

Checking first one pocket, then the other, Duncan finally located it.

"What are you doing?" Madison stared at the blade as he opened the knife.

"I've got to cut the cord."

The irony hit him. Something that had been used, in all likelihood, by its previous owner to cut life short was now being used to allow new life to continue.

Duncan figured it was a good deed by proxy. Taking out the cigarette lighter he kept as a reminder of a habit he had conquered, he sterilized the blade as best he could, then quickly made the cut.

The baby cried for the first time, whether from pain or just because he felt like it, Duncan hadn't a clue. Uncomfortable, he hoped it was the latter.

Very carefully, he closed the knife again, staring at the duo before him. Something he couldn't put a name to was struggling within his chest to get out. But since he couldn't recognize it, he had no idea what he was feeling and only a vague idea as to why.

Unconsciously, Madison began to rock in response to the baby's cries, innately trying to soothe his distress. She stared at the infant in awed wonder, a myriad of formless, faceless emotions volleying through her.

Her child, this was her child.

Hers and who else's?

Her head ached, refusing to allow her to pursue a single thought to any end.

"Thank you," she mouthed to Duncan, the words barely an audible whisper on her breath.

Duncan merely nodded in response, not having much energy for anything more himself. For a moment, he sat back and just looked at Madison and her baby. Looked and tried to absorb the feeling that accompanied the sight.

Damn, but that felt good, he thought. Good to be a part of something that was life affirming instead of life terminating. The ultimate goal of his job, of his department was to successfully block and ban any drugs from coming into the country. But in trying to protect the lives of people—of adolescents—he would never see, he'd had to kill people or see people killed. Whether they were scum or not, it was something that drained a man.

He hadn't realized how moved something like birth could leave him. Very gently, he pressed the tip of his finger against the baby's tightly clenched fist. The next moment, his finger was held fast.

As was something inside of him.

Abruptly, the moment was shattered. High beams suddenly sliced through the fog like twin lasers determined to cut away any obstacle.

Duncan swung around, looking in the direction of the beams. Headlights. It wasn't beyond life's perverse sense of humor to find a way to cut all three of them down a moment after bathing them in one of the few miracles that were still left in this world.

His heart lodged somewhere between his chest and

his throat, and he leaped from the car. He ran in front of the lights, determined to somehow stop the oncoming vehicle before it plowed into them.

Behind him, he heard Madison cry out his name, pleading that he remain. Whether she was afraid for his sake or her own, or perhaps the baby's, he didn't know. It made no difference. The next moment he could distinguish the front end of a police car moving cautiously toward them, a cat uncertain whether it was stalking a prey or an adversary.

Relief washed over him.

Looked like the cavalry had finally arrived, late but at least here. Duncan waved his arms before him, shouting long before he could make out the face of the driver in the squad car.

"Stop! I've got a woman who just gave birth in the car. I need an ambulance."

Once the call was put in, the ambulance arrived with amazing speed, given the weather conditions. It turned out that there was one in the area, returning from a run to Harris Memorial, the closest hospital. Within fifteen minutes of the squad car's arrival, Madison and her son were being gently eased onto a stretcher.

One of the paramedics walked over to Duncan and held out his bloodied jacket. "I figure this must be yours." There was sympathy in the man's voice.

Duncan took it from him gingerly. The jacket's condition, he judged, would have driven any self-respecting dry cleaner into a hair-pulling frenzy. He saw no reason to attempt to salvage it once he took the contents out of the pockets.

"Looks like it was a real good jacket." The paramedic shook his head over the apparent loss.

Duncan shrugged. The jacket was the least of his concerns. Money and the fine things it could buy had never been a problem for him. His problems lay in different directions. "Couldn't be helped."

He saw the policeman who'd radioed for the ambulance looking dubiously at Madison's vehicle. The car's nose was all but butted up against the side of the hill. If the police towed it away, there was no telling where it might ultimately end up. Duncan knew all about snafus. There was no need to run the risk of an added complication. Madison had enough to deal with for one night.

Duncan strode over to the policeman before the latter could put in a call to the dispatcher. "I'll take care of it, Officer."

Eyes that looked almost black in the limited light shifted from one car to the other. "Can't drive both of them."

"Not that one at any rate." Duncan nodded at Madison's car. Unless he missed his guess, it was going to need some work before it was serviceable again. "I'll have someone come to tow it away." It would be his gift to Madison. Then, because the policeman still looked doubtful, Duncan added, "It's safely off the road, and there are flares around it."

The rationale was acceptable and the policeman wasn't going to be difficult, Duncan was sure. Not with someone from the DEA.

The policeman nodded, then glanced toward the ambulance. The stretcher was being placed into the back of the vehicle. He jerked a thumb toward it. "You going with her?"

Duncan hadn't had any intentions of going with Madison. He'd done his duty by her and it was time to get back to his own life. But before he could say anything, he saw the expression on Madison's face. She was looking at him, as if silently asking him to come.

So, for reasons he couldn't begin to understand, the matter was taken out of his hands. What the hell? He hadn't made any particular plans for this evening. He might as well come along to see if there were any loose ends that needed tying up. Maybe he could even call her husband for her.

"Yeah," he said, nodding, "I'm going with her."

As the ambulance door slammed shut, Duncan got in behind the wheel of his car and turned on the ignition. It looked like his adventure was to continue for a little while longer, he mused.

Three

Duncan.

The name beat like a throbbing refrain through her mind.

He was standing there, framed by the bright lights of the emergency room behind him, when the rear ambulance doors opened again. She saw him just as the two paramedics lifted her out.

Relief washed over Madison, as real, as tangible as a sweet breath of cool air.

She supposed it was insane to hope that the Good Samaritan with the shoulder holster and the gentle hands would put himself out even further and follow her to the hospital, but all during the ride, Madison had hoped that he would. Hoped, because in this incredibly new world she found spinning around her, Duncan was her oldest acquaintance, her oldest ally.

And maybe, just maybe, her oldest friend.

Aluminum legs tucked beneath the stretcher snapped into position, transforming it into a gurney. The next moment, Madison felt herself being sped toward the hospital emergency room entrance. Her stomach churned in response.

Duncan was beside her as she and her son passed through the electronic doors. There was a comfort in that, a comfort in having him close by. Did that make her weak, seeking shelter in his familiar presence?

Madison didn't know. All she knew was that she was grateful that he had decided to come.

She wasn't sure if she tried to lift her hand to him and failed, or only thought about doing it. But her mouth did curve as she looked up at him. He had a gruff manner, but his eyes were nice. Kind. Just as he was, beneath the rough exterior. Because he was here when he could be anywhere.

"You came," she whispered.

It was impossible to ignore the fact that there were people everywhere. Duncan didn't want Madison making anything of his impulsive action. After all, a man had a right to see something through to the end if he wanted to. Or at least to an end that satisfied him.

He lifted his shoulder in a half shrug. "Couldn't help myself. Always wanted to know what it felt like to be an ambulance chaser."

The baby stirred, drawing Duncan's eyes from Madison's face to the small, bundled figure. Now that he was actually here, Duncan felt a little foolish. There was no real reason for him to have tagged along. It wasn't as if she were a friend or meant anything to him. The woman was bound to have people coming by to see her as soon as she made the necessary calls. There was no need for him to be here.

But looking at her face as they entered the hospital, Duncan decided that maybe there was. At least to begin with. He could start the ball rolling for her. She hardly looked as if she were up to making phone calls right now. He could do that for her. Someone had to be worried about her. He knew that he would've been, had she been part of his life, pregnant and traveling alone the way she was.

Duncan figured he could spare the few extra minutes. He shoved his hands into his pockets. "Anyone you want me to notify for you?"

The paramedics brought the gurney to a halt a few feet inside the hospital. Madison was grateful that the unsettling motion had ceased. She opened her mouth to answer, hoping that perhaps the response would come automatically.

But it didn't. Nothing came out. No names readily sprang to her tongue.

Or her mind.

She sighed, trying not to let the hopelessness swallow her. "No one I know of."

Duncan's eyes narrowed. The same expression that had been on her face when he'd asked her her name was back. She looked lost, bewildered, as if his question had ripped up all the boundary signs in her life.

She was too old to be a runaway. But not to be running from something. Or someone. "You're by yourself?" he asked.

Whether she was or not, Madison didn't know. But it felt that way. She noticed a look of pity on the face of one of the paramedics. She tried to ignore him. "I guess I am."

If he'd ever heard a lonelier-sounding statement, Duncan couldn't remember it.

A heavyset nurse, her years of service well documented amid the lines on her face, approached and politely but firmly nudged Duncan aside as she assumed his space. Duncan had a feeling that despite her friendly manner, the woman would stand for no nonsense. That was fine with him; she could take over.

The nurse's gray eyes shifted from the sleeping baby to Madison. "A new mother I see."

Mother. Madison sighed. The word evoked no memories, no maternal feelings. It hung elusively in space, a brass ring for her to catch the next revolution the carousel made. Maybe.

Madison concentrated on what she knew and turned her head toward Duncan. "He delivered my son," she told the nurse.

The woman, whose small name tag proclaimed her to be Angie Browne, R.N., nodded her approval. She spared Duncan a glance.

"Nice job. I guess there's nothing left for us to do except clean you two up and see that you get a good night's rest." When she looked at the paramedics, it was with the easy air of familiarity. "We'll take it from here, boys. See you next run."

As they withdrew, Angie got down to business. "Is your doctor affiliated with Harris Memorial, honey?"

More questions. Madison tried to think, but no seedlings pushed through the murky barrenness. "I don't know."

The answer didn't seem to surprise Angie. "Well, tell me his name and I'll probably be able to tell you if he is or isn't." The perfect smile widened, taking in Duncan as well as Madison and the sleeping infant at her breast. "Been here eighteen years and there's hardly anyone I don't recognize, at least by name."

The edginess, temporarily held at bay throughout Madison's labor, reemerged now to lay siege to her. She could feel the tightness in her chest. Her head was already throbbing. "I don't know," she repeated.

The words sounded so hollow, so overwhelmingly desolate. Why didn't she know? How could she have been a whole person before and such a shell of one now?

Her eyes darted toward Duncan with a silent plea for help.

The patience in Angie's voice sounded boundless. "You don't know his name?" she prodded gently.

"I don't know if I have one—" Madison bit her lower lip. It was so frustrating, so bewildering. The words spilled out, along with the confusion. "I came to after the accident and couldn't remember anything. *Anything,*" she emphasized.

Angie's eyebrow rose as she looked to the man at her elbow for an explanation. "Accident?"

Duncan recited the particulars in the quick, detached manner of a man accustomed to getting to the bare essentials without fanfare. He tried not to dwell on the thought that her loss of memory was all his fault.

"Her car was stalled on the road. I didn't see it in the fog until it was almost too late. The two cars barely touched but—" He shrugged, the helplessness of the gesture aggravating him. "But it was enough. Madison hit her head."

Guilt nibbled at him. If he had only seen Madison's car a split second earlier, all this could have been avoided. She might not even have gone into labor.

And he would have never held a seconds-old infant in his hands. Now that it had happened, he knew he would have regretted missing that experience. Under the circumstances, he supposed that made him a sentimental fool. It was a revelation. He'd never thought of himself as being sentimental.

Duncan watched Angie examine the gash on Madison's forehead with quick, competent movements. One of the paramedics had cleaned it during the ride over, but her forehead was still swollen beneath the fringe of blond hair.

"Won't leave a scar." Angie patted her arm gently. "But you'll have a festival of colors there for a while." The grandmotherly smile was understanding. "Don't worry, honey, cases of temporary amnesia are more common than you'd think."

"Temporary?" Madison clutched at the word, a flimsy life preserver in the dark, fathomless sea she found herself in. "Then it'll go away?"

The desperate hope in her voice twisted at Duncan's heart, surprising him. He'd heard men pleading for their lives and it had affected him less than Madison's question did. But then, he rationalized, an entirely different caliber of person had been involved.

And what made him think she was so unique?

Duncan ran his hand along the back of his neck. He was tired and he had nothing to base his impression on but a gut instinct. Sometimes, that was enough.

"Like as not, it'll disappear in a few days. A few weeks at most," Angie was saying to Madison. "We'll run a few tests on you just to make sure nothing else is going on." Her expression stiffened slightly as she saw a smartly attired woman approaching them. She lowered her voice so that only Madison and Duncan heard. "Now would be the

time to get your memory back if you could do it at
will.''

Duncan followed the nurse's line of vision. A for-
tyish woman was walking toward them, hugging a
clipboard to her navy blue double-breasted jacket.
Clipboards notoriously meant paperwork. He'd never
liked paperwork.

"Why?" He looked at the nurse. "Is there a problem?"

Angie spoke slowly, calmly. "Not for me, but ad-
ministration likes their forms filled out and that's one
of their prize watchdogs."

"Insurance forms," Duncan specified. It wasn't a
question.

"Afraid so." By her expression, it was evident to
Duncan that the nurse felt for Madison. "If she
doesn't know who she is—" A glimmer of hope rose
in the gray eyes as Angie looked down at Madison.
"Do you have a purse with you?"

She scanned the outline beneath the blanket for a
telltale lump.

Duncan had scoured the interior of Madison's car
while they'd waited for the ambulance to arrive. In
his experience, every woman had some sort of purse.
He'd been surprised when none turned up. That
meant either Madison was absentminded to begin
with, or she had left in a hurry. Her advanced condition pointed to the latter.

"No purse," he told Angie.

But her name had to be on the registration, he
suddenly realized. Why hadn't he thought of that before? The labor and delivery might have been out of
the realm of things he was trained to handle, but that

was no excuse. He was supposed to be able to think on his feet in the worst situations.

Duncan made a mental note to check out the vehicle on his way home. He would put off calling a towing service until he had a chance to look through the car. If she was running from something, maybe there was some sort of clue that he'd missed the first time.

"And who do we have here?" the strawberry blonde with the clipboard asked as she beamed down at Madison and her son.

"My name is Madison." That was all she could offer. There was still only a void where her last name should have been.

Madison looked too exhausted to field questions she had no answers for, Duncan thought. If he had examined his reaction more closely, he would have been the first to be surprised that there was a layer of protectiveness to it.

His line of work necessitated making split-second decisions every waking hour while on the job. The instinct carried over into whatever was left of his private life. Taking out his wallet, Duncan handed the blonde a platinum credit card.

"Here, why don't you just put whatever she needs on my card?"

Surprised, the woman took the card into her hand. Her eyes swept over Duncan with no small appreciation at what she saw.

"Well, this is highly unorthodox, Mr.—" Needing a name, she lowered her eyes to the card he'd given her and read, "Mr. MacNeill. We generally accept insurance cards, not charge cards. There are forms to fill out, histories to enter—"

Tired, Duncan was fresh out of patience for the second time in little more than an hour. His low, steely voice cut through the social amenities. "She can't remember her history, Ms. Mason." He lifted the name from the chief administrator's badge the woman wore on her left shoulder. "She can't remember who she is. Except for her first name," he clarified. Pamela Mason's mouth fell open, giving her an incredibly stupefied look that grated on Duncan's nerves. "The lady's been in an accident and delivered a baby, all in the last hour. Why don't you just cut her some slack? When she remembers who she is, she'll tell you." Struggling to rein in his temper, Duncan glanced toward Madison for confirmation. "Right?"

But Madison had focused on something else he'd just said. "I can't let you pay for me."

The protest caught him off guard. People were always out for money, getting someone else to foot the bill for them. It had been a long time since he'd been moved to generosity. Why was she trying to be difficult?

"We'll work something out," he told her tersely.

"I won't take charity," Madison insisted, gathering the baby closer to her.

It was a commendable attribute. Self-sufficiency always was. That didn't stop him from wanting to shake her until she talked sense.

"Excuse us."

His phrase was aimed at the nurse and the hospital administrator. Quickly, Duncan moved Madison's gurney to one side, away from the women. He lowered his voice. This wasn't going to be a debate. In his mind, the matter was already settled. He just had to make that clear to Madison.

"Right now, you don't have a whole lot of options going for you." Duncan ground the words out. "Like it or not, you're going to have to accept 'charity' for the time being. The only choice you have is the kind of charity you pick. Mine or some institution's." He didn't give her time to consider. "Trust me, you won't like the difference." Duncan looked at the baby. "And neither will he."

Something small and stubborn reared its head within Madison. Tired though she was, she wanted to argue with him. She inherently sensed, *knew,* that she didn't accept charity. Ever.

Yet, he was right. She had no choice. For the baby's sake, she had to agree. Relenting, she nodded reluctantly. "I guess you've come to my rescue twice today."

Duncan wasn't about to let her get started on thanking him again. He just wanted to get the hell out of here and check out her car. Puzzles always ate away at him, and right now, Madison-with-the-bright-green-eyes-and-no-last-name was a puzzle.

"All in a day's work," he said cryptically.

He moved the gurney back toward the two women. Angie was talking to a wan-looking man in a lab coat. Was it just him, Duncan wondered, or were doctors getting younger-looking these days? Lately, he'd been feeling twice his age. Maybe his superior was right. Maybe he did need a vacation. Even Stringburne had to be right once in a while, he supposed.

The next moment, Duncan found himself facing an awestruck administrator. Pamela Mason looked at his credit card again before she raised her eyes to his face.

The card had an unlimited ceiling so he doubted the problem involved money. "Something wrong?" he asked gamely.

"No..." Ms. Mason caught herself in a stammer and began again. "Are you *the* Duncan MacNeill? The one from the newspapers?" The question came at him breathlessly, as she anticipated his answer.

For the umpteenth time, Duncan cursed overzealous reporters and the public's hunger for vicarious excitement and details.

"I don't know. I never read the newspaper," he replied coolly. He could see that wasn't enough for the woman. He shifted his attention toward the nurse and figured she was the more levelheaded of the two. "Look, it's been a long day for both of us and I—"

But the hospital administrator wasn't put off that easily. She moved so that she was between Duncan and the others, convinced she was right and determined to get him to admit it.

"Yes, you *are*. You are the man from the newspaper." Excited, she turned to the nurse beside her. "This is Duncan MacNeill, Angie. He's the one who broke up that drug ring. You know, the undercover agent they had on the front page. Remember, I said he—"

Abruptly, Ms. Mason stopped. Whatever she'd said earlier was now quickly glossed over. "Never mind," she said primly to Duncan, then sought refuge in her work. "There'll be no problem keeping your friend here."

It wasn't difficult to pick up on what was being left unsaid. The woman had obviously remembered

that the article had made a point of mentioning that
he was the grandson of Thomas MacNeill, the founder of MacNeill's Sweets. And, since he was his parents' only heir, that made him exceedingly wealthy.
He chafed at the implication, even though it was true.

Duncan focused on the positive aspect of the
woman's pandering. "Good. Then there won't be a
problem giving Madison a private room." He knew
if he had to stay in a hospital, that would be the only
way he could endure it. His eyes met Madison's
briefly. "I think she's earned her privacy after this
evening."

Ms. Mason was only too happy to comply. "Anything you say, Mr. MacNeill."

Money and notoriety had its privileges, he supposed, but Duncan still found it grating. Maybe he
would have found the flip side equally annoying, but
somehow he doubted it. Satisfied that he'd done all
that he could for Madison and her son, Duncan began
to leave, when an afterthought occurred to him. Madison still needed a doctor. He thought of Sheila.

"By the way, you might want to call Sheila Pollack in to see her." He made the suggestion to the
nurse.

The older woman looked surprised. Dr. Pollack
was a gynecologist. "You know Dr. Pollack?"

Duncan didn't see any need to tell either woman
that he and Sheila had dated years ago. The relationship had been more platonic than anything else. He'd
been too much the angry rebel for it to have gone
any other way at the time. But they had remained
friends and their paths still crossed from time to time.
He'd heard she was a good doctor. Knowing Sheila,
he wasn't surprised.

"Yes, I know her. I'd appreciate it if you called her in. Tell her to bill me for her services. She knows where to send it."

The knowing glance exchanged between the nurse and administrator didn't escape him. He figured the rumor would be all over the hospital by morning: Prominent doctor involved with wealthy DEA agent. He almost laughed out loud at the absurdity of the thought, but he knew how people's minds operated. Duncan had no doubt that Sheila could competently handle any gossip that their acquaintance might spontaneously generate. He only hoped her husband had a sense of humor.

Duncan decided he'd already lingered far too long. It was time to get going before something else happened to make him stay the night.

He was tempted just to walk out, but the look on Madison's face stopped him. Again. Why did he feel as if he were setting a homeless waif out on the street? Nothing could be further from the truth. So why couldn't he shake that feeling?

"You'll be okay," he assured her gruffly.

"Sure."

The answer came much too fast to be sincere, but there wasn't anything he could do about that, or about the doubts she had to be feeling. He wasn't a social worker, he was a DEA agent. That made him accustomed to dealing with unsavory characters, not newborns and their mothers.

The baby made a squeaky noise. Looking down at him, Duncan realized that he was asleep. Unable to help himself, he lingered a moment longer, knowing if he had half a brain, he would've already been three-quarters of the way home by now.

"What are you going to call him?" A man should know the name of the child he helped bring into the world, Duncan reasoned, even if he was never going to see him again. Very lightly, he passed his hand over the soft, downy head, barely touching it.

Madison looked at the sleeping child, then raised her eyes to Duncan's.

"Neil," she decided. She added her smile to her words. "It has a nice ring to it."

Neil. She'd taken his last name and molded it to her son. Something touched him, even though he tried to prevent it.

"None that I ever noticed." No, that wasn't strictly true, Duncan amended. He got along well with his uncle Thomas. If it hadn't been for Thomas, he knew he wouldn't have had any sense of family whatsoever while he was growing up. He had certainly never gotten any from his own parents, both of whom had passions that took them in directions that were far from him.

"You might want to reconsider your choice," Duncan suggested.

But Madison only shook her head. She'd already made up her mind. Duncan MacNeill had come to her rescue, hers and her son's. Without him, neither one of them might be here right now. Naming her son after him was the least she could do. "I like Neil."

Duncan shrugged. "Suit yourself."

Hands braced on either side, Angie positioned herself at the foot of the gurney. "It's time we got you to a room. I'll call ahead to see what we have open. Shouldn't be a problem," she assured Madison. "Maternity's been rather slow lately."

"Not from where I'm standing," Duncan commented, looking at his new namesake. "Take care of yourself," he told Madison.

Her eyes said things to him her lips couldn't under the present circumstances. "Thank you, Duncan. For everything."

The look in her eyes made him feel restless. It only meant it was time to go.

"Yeah." He turned on his heel, ready to make his escape. He didn't get far.

"Oh, Mr. MacNeill," Ms. Mason called after him. She hurried to catch up before he could make good his retreat. "Would you mind signing this, please?" She maneuvered the clipboard in front of him. "It's just a formality."

Duncan looked at the form attached to the clipboard. The only thing his father had ever taught him, other than how to make a perfect martini, was that so-called "formalities" had a way of making you pay. Duncan made it a practice of always knowing what it was he was signing. Curbing his impatience, he scanned the page quickly before writing his name on the designated line.

Handing the clipboard back to the woman, Duncan left the hospital. For good, he thought.

Four

Duncan frowned thoughtfully at the piece of paper in his hand. The fog outside the car window was as dense as it had been two hours ago, and misty fingers were burrowing their way inside the vehicle where Madison had given birth. Duncan had found the car just where they'd left it. True to his word, the policeman hadn't had it towed away.

Sitting on the passenger side, Duncan had turned on the overhead light before opening the glove compartment. The registration slip was the only thing he found inside. He'd thought of the condition of his own glove compartment and marveled at the lack of clutter.

Reading the name on the solitary sheet, he discovered that the car was registered to an Edward Jackson. There was a Santa Barbara address beneath the man's name. Santa Barbara was more than two hundred miles from Bedford. Had Madison been down here on a visit when she'd had the accident?

Duncan fingered the registration. The faint light illuminating the interior cast surreal, misshapen shadows around him, darkening his mood. Jackson was either her husband or her father. In either case, Madison and her son had someone in their lives. They weren't his concern anymore, not even peripherally. They would be taken care of.

He got out of the car and slammed the door shut. Locking it, he pocketed Madison's keys and slipped the registration into his other pocket.

He'd call Ed Jackson as soon as he got to his house and tracked down the man's number. Madison and Neil weren't his problem any longer, he thought again. He waited for a sense of freedom to hit.

But all he felt was the fog as it closed its dank and clammy arms around him.

"Who?" the reedy voice on the other end of the line asked. Jackson, an older man by the sound of his voice, seemed genuinely confused.

Maybe he should've just driven up to Santa Barbara to see the man in person, Duncan thought, instead of getting Jackson's number from Information. Conducting business over the phone was never his first choice, but the drive there and back would have eaten up too much of his time.

"Madison," Duncan repeated, biting back impatience. Unless Madison had stolen the car, Jackson had to be connected to her—if not related—in some way. Why was the man acting as if he'd never heard of her?

"I don't know any Mad—wait, hold on. Sure I do." Duncan could almost see the lightbulb going on over the man's head. "Blond lady? Pregnant enough to be carrying a brass band inside of her?"

The description was crude but generally accurate. And impersonal. Maybe the man wasn't familiar with Madison. "Not anymore."

The roundabout confirmation was enough for Jackson. "Hell, yes, I know her. Sort of," he amended almost immediately, his enthusiasm lowering half a notch. "She bought my car."

That would explain the empty glove compartment and Jackson's initial confusion. It also meant that the man couldn't tell him very much. "When?"

Jackson paused, thinking. "A couple of weeks ago." Disappointment more than surprise echoed in his voice. What Duncan noticed was that it was devoid of any signs of annoyance. "You mean she hasn't sent in the registration paper yet?"

Duncan cursed his shortsightedness. When he found the registration slip, it hadn't occurred to him that the vehicle might have been recently transferred. Moving closer to the lamp on his desk, he flipped the paper over. Sure enough, there, on the back, was Jackson's signature. The illegible scribble beneath it had to belong to Madison. He couldn't make out the last name. He wouldn't have been able to read the first, either, if he hadn't known what it was.

Frustrated, Duncan swallowed another curse. Just his luck, she had handwriting like a doctor. He was going to have to get this to the lab and have someone try to decipher it for him.

"No, she didn't send in the registration." To forestall any lengthy tirade Jackson might let loose, Duncan added, "She's been in an accident."

"An accident?" Duncan thought he detected a slight twang in the startled voice, but he couldn't place it. "She okay?"

"She's fine." He didn't know that for a fact, Duncan realized. It was just an assumption on his part. He supposed the hospital would have called him if something had gone wrong. "But she's lost her memory. Is she a friend of yours?"

There was a wistful chuckle on the other end of the line. "Don't I wish. I don't have any friends who are that classy."

Classy. Yes, he supposed that would be the word to describe her, but Duncan didn't want to listen to a personal narrative of Jackson's life. He just wanted to know how the man happened to meet Madison. "Then how did you—?"

Jackson was way ahead of him. "She answered the ad I placed in the paper about selling my car. Told me she was just passing through and needed a car. I didn't ask her how she came to be in Santa Barbara in the first place and she didn't volunteer the information." The man was turning out to be a huge disappointment, Duncan thought, frustrated. "I did ask her where her mister was, though."

Duncan wasn't sure he followed Jackson's meaning. "Her mister?"

"Yeah, you know, her husband. The baby's father. She said she didn't have one." Jackson sounded sympathetic as he commented, "By the look of her, I figured it was something she regretted, being pregnant and all. Lady like that should have a man in her life."

Well, she'd obviously had one in her life nine months ago, Duncan thought cynically. Had he walked out on her, or was the reverse the case? "Did she tell you her last name?"

"Nope, didn't ask. First name's good enough for me." And then he remembered. "But she wrote it on the back of the registration."

In hieroglyphics, Duncan thought, looking at the pen scratch again. He wondered if that was deliberate on her part.

"Did she give you a personal check?" He could trace the check through Jackson's bank and get her name and address that way. Duncan poised his pencil over the pad on his desk.

"Now, that was the real funny part."

"Funny part?" Duncan had a feeling he wasn't going to be laughing.

"Yeah, she paid me in cash. Twelve hundred dollars, all hundreds. The bills had a funny smell to them, like she'd been saving them in some closed box or something for a long time, you know?

"It was late when she came by, and my missus felt kinda sorry for her, having to drive off at night and all. We told her she could stay until morning, sleep in Jenny's room. Jenny's my youngest. She's gone to college—"

Duncan had a feeling that if he didn't cut Jackson off, the man would go on all night. He tried another line of questioning.

"How did Madison get to your place? Did someone drop her off?" If he had a description to go on, maybe that could lead to more pertinent information.

But all Jackson could offer him was another dead end. "She said she came by bus. Hell of a walk to my place if she did. You say she's all right?"

Duncan was amazed at the genuine concern in the man's voice. If Madison was a stranger to Jackson the way he maintained, she'd certainly aroused a great deal of feeling in an incredibly short amount of time.

"Yes, she's all right." As all right as anyone could be with amnesia. Frustrated, Duncan tossed the pencil aside and rocked back in his chair. He should have been more tolerant of dead ends, given his experience. But he was tired and in no mood for failure. "So there's nothing you can tell me about her?"

"Only that my dog liked her and she seemed kind of nervous." Jackson lowered his voice, as if revealing a secret. "Couldn't really sit still, you know? But I figured in her condition and all, she was entitled."

It wasn't Madison's condition that had made her nervous, Duncan was ready to make book on that. She was running from something. Or to.

Temporarily stymied, Duncan stared at the registration slip on the desk before him. "Thanks for your help, Mr. Jackson. I might be in touch again."

"No problem." Jackson sounded only too happy to help. "Who did you say you were again?"

"Duncan MacNeill. I'm with the DEA," he added before Jackson could ask.

There was a long pause on the other end, as if the man were digesting the significance of the identifying letters.

"She's not in any trouble, is she?" Jackson's voice was hushed, respectful. Duncan wondered if the man was having second thoughts about talking to him. Not that he'd actually said anything.

"None that I know of. Like I said, she lost her memory. I'm just trying to help her piece things together." In a roundabout way, he could have been telling the truth, Duncan thought, although he felt no need to rationalize his actions.

"That's very decent of you. Let me know if there's anything I can do. The missus and I really liked her."

"Right." Well, this had gotten him nowhere.

"Goodbye." Hanging up, Duncan stared off into space.

Decent.

He hadn't heard that assessment applied to him in a long time. Two years. Probably longer. But at least two years. Two years was the length of time he'd been undercover, painstakingly arranging the strands of the intricate web that eventually closed around Carlos Montoya and the multimillion-dollar drug cartel he headed. All told, one hundred and twenty men had been brought in so far, and the tally was still rising. Only Montenegro, Montoya's first in command, was conspicuously missing.

No, *decent* wasn't a word he was acquainted with any longer. Duncan doubted if it could be applied to him in any case. His motives weren't particularly noble. He was just trying to attach a last name to Madison and satisfy his own mushrooming curiosity.

But rather than satisfy it, all he'd managed to do was arouse it further. Methodically, he prioritized his questions. Habit had him doing it mentally rather than on paper. Leaving anything in writing could have been detrimental to the state of his health these last two years.

It was a habit that was going to be hard to break, he thought, picking up the pencil again. Equally difficult would be refraining from the temptation to look over his shoulder. Since there'd been no one to watch his back when he'd gone under, he'd practically had to develop a second set of eyes in the back of his head.

In the everyday world, that was called paranoia. In the one he'd lived in, it was called survival.

Duncan rotated his shoulders and got down to

business, writing the questions in the order of their importance. Who was the woman fate had flung into his life tonight? Was she running from someone? And if so, who? Why? And why did she have twelve hundred dollars in her possession? Most people carried around checkbooks and plastic, not large quantities of cash.

Duncan put the pencil down again. Maybe he was making something out of nothing.

"Sometimes, Duncan," his uncle Thomas was fond of saying, "a duck is just a duck and nothing more." Was he trying to turn a duck into something else, something sinister? The question almost succeeded in amusing him.

The phone rang, shattering his concentration. Swearing, Duncan debated letting his machine pick up, then decided against it. The call might be important and he didn't feel like playing games or picking up too late once he heard the caller's voice. The entire conversation would wind up being recorded by his answering machine.

He lifted the receiver on the third ring. "Mac-Neill."

There was a slight pause before he heard the low, throaty laugh.

"I wasn't sure you still had this number. I should have realized you were a creature of habit." He tried to place the voice but she told him before he managed to make a match. "Duncan, it's Sheila Pollack. The overworked gynecologist you referred that amnesia victim to, in case you don't remember."

"I remember." A hint of a smile lifted his lips as he settled back in the chair. He tucked the receiver against his shoulder and his neck. Duncan remembered a great deal about Sheila, all of it pleasant. She kept late hours, he thought. "So, how have you been?"

"Busy." Even now, he could detect a slightly harried note in her voice. "The same can be said for you, I guess. I've seen the newspapers."

He toyed with the registration slip, moving it to one side, then back again with his fingertips. He wondered if it would do any good to run a check on Ed Jackson and see what turned up. The man could have been lying.

"Apparently so has everyone else. The damn reporter who broke the story in San Diego and got my picture, blew what was left of my cover. I'm out of undercover work, probably permanently." He banked down the regret that came with the words, but not before a glimmer of bitterness found him.

Married to an investigative reporter whose assignments occasionally took him to places best left undisturbed, Sheila was sympathetic only up to a point. "I guess you'll have to find some other way to risk your neck. Or have you found it already?"

Duncan paid closer attention to the conversation. "What are you talking about?"

"The new mama," she reminded him. "Madison. Are you two connected?"

The thing that had always attracted him to Sheila was her mind. It was always working. But the connection wasn't what she thought. "Only in so far as I helped her deliver her baby."

Sheila laughed at the thought. She could envision Duncan in a great many roles, but being a midwife was not one of them. "Well, well, well, I had no idea you had such hidden talents, Duncan." Her voice softened. It was a paradox that amid all the glamour surrounding his private life and the dangerous life-and-death aspects of his work, Duncan had spent too many years alone. "She speaks very highly of you."

The mild interest Sheila's comment evoked passed quickly. "From what I gather, I'm the only one she can speak of." Or maybe, given what he was piecing together, that was just an elaborate act. "*Does* she have amnesia, Sheila?"

"I deal with the other end, remember?" Sheila reminded him. "Besides, amnesia isn't something you can verify with a simple test. The best you can do is conclude what might have caused it. In Madison's case, she does have a nasty bump on the head that more than likely is responsible for her condition. I've had a few tests run on her. All negative. There's no evidence of a concussion, either." She paused, knowing better than to ask what was up. Duncan had been closemouthed for as long as she'd known him. "I tend to believe people when they tell me things."

"I don't."

Sheila's laugh was short, but not unkind. "Yes, I know. You always were a cynic." The hour was late and she had to be getting home. She wanted to see Rebecca, if only to peek in on her sleeping daughter. "Anyway, I called to tell you that except for her memory loss and a few miscellaneous bruises here and there, Madison appears to be in good health."

"Bruises?" Instantly alert, his mind began churning out half a dozen scenarios. "You mean there's more than just the bump on her head?" Something else he'd missed, he reproached himself.

"There're a few bruises on her arms. They look

relatively fresh." There could be a myriad of reasons behind them, but human nature pointed toward the worst. Abuse. "I figure that's more your jurisdiction than mine."

He was already involved more than he should have been, Duncan thought. "I'm not a cop, Sheila, I'm with the DEA."

He wasn't fooling her. "You were always a cop, Duncan. You have a cop's soul." Sheila changed the subject. "So tell me, now that you can't dress down and hang out with sleazy people anymore, when are you coming over for dinner? Slade would love to meet a man from my past." Mercifully, Slade didn't have a jealous bone in his body—only curious ones.

"Your husband's a reporter, right?" Duncan didn't remember which newspaper the man worked for, but he remembered that Slade Garrett was an investigative reporter. He had little use for reporters no matter what their qualifying title.

Sheila was aware of how Duncan felt. It was a given, but in this case, it didn't apply. "Yes, but he's one of the good guys. Really."

If Sheila'd married Garrett, Duncan supposed that the man would have to be. But voluntarily spending an evening in the company of a reporter was something he was going to have to think about before agreeing to. "I'll get back to you on that, Sheila."

"You'd better." She really wanted the two men to get together. They had more in common than Duncan might think, except that Slade was totally at peace with himself and his surroundings. Duncan had yet to declare a truce with himself, even an uneasy one. "Remember, I know where you live. By the way, I know you're not much on socializing, but are you planning to visit Madison?''

''Why?'' Duncan's suspicious nature, honed by necessity, took over.

That was typical Duncan, Sheila thought. Never an answer before he knew all the details. ''Because I think she could stand a friend right now.''

He wasn't about to get personally involved with the woman. ''Then talk to her. You're a woman. Women talk more freely to other women.''

''Sometimes,'' she allowed. ''But I'm so busy now, even Slade has to make an appointment to see me.'' The teasing tone faded. ''Go see her, Duncan. You can probably do her more good than I can.''

It was an odd thing for Sheila to say. Why should talking to him mean anything more to Madison than talking to anyone else? ''What's that supposed to mean?''

Sheila sighed. It was a wonder civilization had advanced so far when men were so dense. Since he couldn't see it, for now she left the obvious unsaid. ''Well, you can help her find her identity.''

''Oh.'' For a moment, he'd thought that Sheila was suggesting something else. Something clearly out of left field. But that was ridiculous. Sheila was far too sensible to try to push Madison and him together. ''Maybe.'' Playing his hand close to the vest was second nature to him. Duncan saw no point in telling Sheila he'd already begun to set wheels in motion to try to discover who Madison really was. ''I'll see.''

That was the best she could get out of him and Sheila knew it. The man never made promises. ''You do that, Duncan. You see.''

* * *

In the end, it wasn't Sheila's prodding that brought Duncan to Madison's room the next afternoon. Or even his own curiosity. It was, instead, the memory of the way he'd felt holding the baby in his hands, the feeling that had washed over him, knowing he was the very first person to hold Neil. Like it or not, that moment, that feeling had created a bond between the infant and him. One that Duncan knew would remain with him all the days of his life.

He'd wrestled with all three—Sheila's urging, his feelings, and his curiosity—for the better part of the morning before giving in. He figured looking in on Madison was better than plowing through all the paperwork that the drug bust had generated for him. Taking an extended lunch, he'd driven over to the hospital before anything came up to make him change his mind.

Just before he reached the bank of elevators in Harris Memorial, Duncan passed a gift shop. Habit, ingrained in him from the days when he was a child and it had actually meant something, had him looking to see if the large blue box of chocolates displayed in the window had the MacNeill insignia on it.

It did. Leaning against the two-pound box was a miniature baseball glove and ball.

Duncan didn't believe in omens, but he'd survived too long dealing with the denizens of the world that comprised life's underbelly not to have amassed a few superstitions along the way. He bought the box as well as the glove and ball.

When he entered her room, he found Madison asleep. For the first time, he took a good look at her.

Without pain contorting her face, she was very pretty. Perhaps even beautiful, although her features weren't those of a high-paid model. It was the kind of face that might have fit very well into a Currier & Ives setting.

She looked younger than he remembered.

Duncan stood a few steps shy of the doorway, debating whether to remain or leave. He didn't feel he had the right to wake her. Madison had been so incredibly exhausted last night. Sleep would do her far more good than he could. Maybe even coming here right now wasn't all that great an idea.

He looked down at the box of chocolates and then at the ball and glove he held in his other hand. He wasn't about to bring those home with him. Moving softly, he crossed to her bed and placed the box and gifts on top of the small, mobile table that was between her and the wall.

Madison opened her eyes and looked directly at him. Duncan stopped where he was, his retreat aborted. He hadn't realized how green her eyes were. They were like two emerald crystals, gleaming.

"Hi." The emotionless greeting sounded awkward to his own ear.

Madison blinked first once, then again, waiting for Duncan to disappear. When he didn't, a wide smile emerged. *He'd come.*

Pressing the control on the side rail, she raised the back of the bed until it eased her into a semiupright position.

"Hi," she answered. "I thought maybe I was dreaming again."

Duncan narrowed in on the telling word. "Again?"

Her smile turned shy as she nodded. "I dreamed about you. It's a little hazy now," she admitted, "but I think there were boxes of chocolate in it."

Someone must have told her. Or was she just putting him on? Looking at her, he would have said she was completely without guile. But he knew better than to be guided by appearances, even appearances as innocent-looking as hers.

"There usually are." He moved the table until the wheels slid under her bed.

She saw the gifts then. Something warm moved inside of her. He'd brought her a gift. And something for the baby. Touched, she read the gold lettering across the top of the box. She was confused when she looked up at him. "You make your own chocolate?"

"Not personally." The bewildered expression on her face almost made him laugh. Hadn't she ever heard of MacNeill's Sweets? "My grandfather, Thomas MacNeill, started the company."

The information seemed to make no impression on Madison. At least, not the kind he had become accustomed to. Learning of his connection to the Fortune 500 company, most women would almost immediately begin fawning on him. The desire to be associated with money was an irresistible lure. But all Madison did was look amused. "When you were a kid, your dentist bills must have been huge."

"I don't like chocolate." It was a taste he had deliberately unacquired. Not that it had made a difference to either parent. He doubted his father even noticed.

"You're kidding." To be surrounded by chocolate and not want any seemed beyond comprehension to her. Madison slid the gold ribbon from the box and removed the lid. The rich scent of dark chocolate wafted up to greet her, stirring her appetite.

"I love chocolate." She raised her head as the words echoed back to her. Her eyes, widening like flowers blooming in an open field beneath the sun, met his. "I love chocolate."

The excitement in her voice was unmistakable. And not without charm, Duncan caught himself thinking.

"Duncan, I remembered something about myself!"

Five

The expression on Madison's face captivated him. There was no other word for it. He was held prisoner by the pure excitement in her eyes, the soft, breathless note in her voice. And oddly enough, he realized that it wasn't entirely against his will.

Moving closer, he was warmed by the smile that radiated from her eyes. If he wasn't in such control of his emotions, he would have found her infectious. "What else do you remember?"

Amnesia didn't conform to specified guidelines. Maybe, in her particular case, they were on the brink of a domino effect. One fact would trigger another until everything came rushing back to her. But he could see as soon as he asked the question that what she had remembered was an isolated fact. It touched off nothing.

The spark of excitement extinguished right before his eyes. It was ridiculous to feel that something had been taken from him, yet Duncan couldn't shake the sensation.

Her slender shoulders rose and fell beneath the hospital gown. She tugged up one side as the blue-and-white material, faded from too many washings, began to slide off.

"That's it." He could hear the sadness she felt struggling to get out and take over. "Just my name and that I like chocolate." The laugh was small and rueful. "Not much to go on."

For some reason he didn't fully understand, Duncan felt compelled to give Madison something to hang on to. Moving the overstuffed burgundy chair in the corner closer to her bed, he sat down. "There's a little more than that."

Hope materialized in the green eyes. It amazed Duncan that he could see every thought, every emotion Madison was experiencing. He wasn't accustomed to such openness, not in his work, not in his life. Trained and extremely capable in holding in check and hiding his thoughts and feelings, he was taken aback when confronted with such unabashed honesty. Why shouldn't she be honest? he thought cynically. At this point, the woman was as innocent as the baby she'd given birth to yesterday. Or so she maintained.

There was still a small part of him, held in reserve, that thought this might be an elaborate act for some unknown reason. Maybe she *was* running from something. In that case, anonymity would serve her well.

But though his suspicious nature was generated by years of dealing with people with multiple hidden agendas, something told him that this wasn't the case here. For once, what he saw was most likely all that there was. A very pretty woman with amnesia.

There were probably a dozen logical explanations for the twelve hundred dollars, too, if he really thought about them.

"You've learned something?" Madison was asking him eagerly, taking hold of his wrist. "Do you know who I am?"

Habit had him start to remove her hand, but then

he stopped. What difference did it make, just this once, if he allowed her to hold on to him? Maybe it actually made her feel better. It seemed a simple enough thing to let slide.

Duncan studied her. "Do you remember buying a car from an Edward Jackson in Santa Barbara?"

Madison paused, rolling both the name and the city over in her mind. Neither roused any memories or attached themselves to any thoughts. Very slowly, she shook her head. The light in her eyes waned. "No."

But Duncan wasn't about to give up so quickly. Tenacity was a natural by-product of his line of work. His eyes remained intent on hers. "You don't remember paying cash for the car?"

"Cash?" she repeated in surprise. He hadn't even found a purse in her car, so where would she have gotten enough cash to pay for a car? "How much was it?"

Experience had taught him to qualify information he dispensed if it wasn't firsthand. "Jackson said he sold the car to you for twelve hundred dollars."

Her mouth dropped open. Twelve hundred dollars? In cash? "And I was carrying that much money around with me?"

Questions began multiplying quickly, pushing their way through the dull ache surrounding Madison's head. Where had the money come from and why would she pay cash for a car? If she had that much cash lying around, why hadn't she put it in a bank? She could feel frustration beginning to form. Why didn't any of what Duncan was telling her spark a memory? Why couldn't she remember something more than her name and a fondness for chocolate?

"Apparently you were." The only kind of people Duncan knew who carried that much money were people involved in drug dealing. His mouth hardened as he looked at Madison again.

Damn, wouldn't that be ironic? That Madonna-like face involved in drug dealing. Duncan reserved judgment, leaning forward.

"You don't remember?" he pressed.

He would have liked to think that if she was lying, he'd be able to tell, but the reality of it was that pathological liars were very cool, very good at making a lie seem like the truth.

"No." Her voice was small, befuddled. Frustrated.

Again, his inclination was to believe her. Duncan had nothing to base his feelings on but a gut reaction and even he would have sneered at anyone relying on nothing more than intuition.

"And you don't remember being in Santa Barbara or what you were doing there?"

Why was he looking at her like that? Did he think she'd stolen the money? Madison struggled against the impulse to wad up the sheet beneath her hand. Nerves threatened to get the better of her.

She took a long, cleansing breath, then let it out again. As calmly as possible, she replied, "No. I don't even know what I'm doing *here*." She glanced pointedly around her. "And I don't even know where 'here' is."

Why would she, he realized, if she had amnesia. The name of the city was only noted on signs as you entered and exited city limits. They'd done neither since the accident.

"You're in Newport Beach." He continued to watch her expression closely, but there was no sign of recognition flittering over her face. The name of the city meant nothing to her. He could have said Buenos Aires and gotten the same response.

Or Bogotá? a small voice inside his head whispered. He filed the thought away for future examination.

Distress had taken over the space that enthusiasm had vacated in her eyes. Though Duncan told himself it made no difference to him, it bothered him to see her like this. In the next breath, he found himself in the completely unfamiliar role of comforter.

"These things take time," he assured her. "Sheila called me last night and said you were doing well, all things considered." That name probably didn't mean anything to her, either. "That's—"

Madison was quick to interrupt. "Your friend, the gynecologist. Yes, I remember that."

Remembered, too, how kind the woman had been to her. Despite the late hour, Sheila Pollack had been willing to remain and talk with her if it would make her feel better. Madison had thanked her and told her she was too tired to talk. It had only been partially true.

"There's not a whole lot of things to clutter up my mind right now," Madison explained to Duncan with a resigned smile. Because he'd sent the doctor to her, she added, "She seems very nice."

A corner of his mouth curved slightly. There was no "seems" about it. Everyone had always liked Sheila. When they'd been together, he'd envied the easy way she could make friends. "She is."

And so was he, Madison thought, even though he sounded inaccessible and remote. But his actions spoke louder than his words.

"Duncan—" She paused, not quite sure how to phrase this without embarrassing or, worse, offending him. She fell back on honesty. It was all she had. "I don't know how to thank you."

"No need to thank me." He'd already told her that last night.

"Yes, there is," she insisted with feeling. She wasn't going to let him shrug this off. "I might not be able to remember how old I am, but I do know that your taking care of my hospital bill—temporarily," she emphasized "—is above and beyond what most people would do for someone they didn't know." She took a breath. "It's probably beyond what they would do for someone they *did* know who wasn't directly related to them."

He was surprised at the dead serious determination in her voice. She meant to thank him and she wasn't about to let it slide under the table. A half smile rose in response. "Well, we're not related, that much I can tell you. I know the exact genealogy of my family right down to who stepped off what boat when."

Even if his parents hadn't been enamored with their heritage, there had been splashy magazine articles to remind him that his family tree was incredibly old and well documented.

As if any of that really mattered in the actual scheme of things. But he wasn't prepared for the longing he saw reflected in Madison's eyes at his words.

"I'd settle for knowing my last name." She looked down at her abdomen, her hand fluttering over it. There was still a slight swell left. "And who my husband is," she added in almost a whisper.

There, at least, he could help, if hearsay was to be believed. "You don't have one."

Her head jerked up. "What?" Her eyes fixed hungrily on his. Was he holding something back? "How do you know that?"

Caution, his longtime companion, had him qualifying his words again. "That's what you told Ed Jackson when he asked you about your husband. He said you told him you didn't have one."

He watched her face. Would the news distress her or make no difference? Just what sort of a person was she, when all the layers were stripped away? He was becoming determined to find out.

Madison looked down at her left hand. It was bare. There was no tan line around her ring finger the way there was around her wrist where her watch had been. She'd already removed it this morning on the off chance that the back was engraved. It wasn't. Disappointment met her at every turn she took.

"I had a feeling I didn't have a husband," she confessed.

"Oh?" He found the rueful smile on her lips appealing but didn't dwell on it.

"That's about all I have to go on right now. Feelings." She sighed helplessly, hoping he didn't think she was a fool. "I'm waiting for some sort of feeling of déjà vu."

"And have you felt it?" The question was asked without emotion, without judgment.

Madison hadn't a clue what was going on in Duncan's mind. That made two minds she knew nothing about, she thought ruefully.

"No." She hated the way that sounded, hated the way the word felt on her tongue when she formed it.

No. Negative. Just like her life was right now. A negative of a photograph hidden from her view. What did she have to do to make the colors return? And what was she going to do until they did?

As if he'd read her mind, Duncan asked, "Have you given any thought to what you're going to do once you get out of here?"

He waited for Madison to give him some sort of answer, preferably off the top of her head. Maybe her instincts would take over and unconsciously guide her in a certain direction, to a certain person. It was worth a shot, he thought. The human mind was an incredible storehouse. Nothing was ever forgotten. It was all in there somewhere, her identity, her memories, all tucked away in her brain. All they needed was to find the right key to unlock the closed door.

Had she given any thought to what she would do? His question almost made Madison laugh. It was all she could do to face waking up this morning and finding herself in the same void she'd been in last night. A world filled with emptiness and a great deal of pain, pain from the accident and from giving birth.

"No, I haven't thought about it. Everything is still spinning in my head." But one thing she had thought about. She pressed her lips together. "I meant what I said last night."

He waited for her to elaborate. When she didn't, he asked, "About…?"

She knew this sounded like big talk coming from someone without even a purse. But grandiose or not, she meant every word. "I intend to pay you back, Duncan. Every penny. With interest."

There was passion in her voice. She had pride, that

much was evident. Duncan tried not to pay attention to the heat behind her words. Or the way her breasts rose and fell as she spoke.

At least she remembered how loans worked, he thought. What was it about a brain that made it selectively remember something as trivial as loan interest and yet not allow her to recall who she was and where she lived?

He dismissed her promise as so much rhetoric. Money had never meant anything to him. Not even as a means to an end. It had just always been there, more of a curse than a comfort.

"Don't worry about it."

How could he say that? Madison wondered. Did he think she was the kind of person who just took whatever she could? And how could he afford to pay for all this? He said he was a government agent. They couldn't earn that much money. Not legally, anyway, and she instinctively knew that he would never stoop to something illegal.

"But I am worried about it," she insisted. She glanced around the suite. It looked more like something found in a hotel than a room in a hospital. "This has to be costing you an awful lot of money, not to mention Dr. Pollack's bill—"

"Then don't mention it," Duncan cut in, irritated that he couldn't turn the tide of the conversation. Being thanked was too much like being fawned over. He hated it. "Look, you want to pay me back? Try to remember who you are."

As if she weren't trying with all her might now? "That wouldn't be for you, that would be for me." Madison looked at him, puzzled. She didn't understand why Duncan would concern himself about her identity. She wasn't anything to him. Was she? Was he keeping something back for his own reasons? Her head ached even more. There were just too many questions going unanswered.

"Why is it so important to you that I remember who I am?" she asked.

Though the fact that she had so much cash on her person aroused his suspicions, the reasons for Duncan wanting her to regain her memory went deeper than just professional curiosity. They went straight to guilt.

"Because I'm obviously the one who made you forget." It bothered him to make the admission out loud, but his ethics wouldn't allow him to lie about it. "If I hadn't hit your car, you wouldn't have hit your head and gotten amnesia."

So that was what she saw in his eyes, Madison realized. Guilt. He was blaming himself for this and trying to make amends. She was a guilt trip for him. The thought that he regarded her in such a light caused a wedge of disappointment to wiggle in.

She absolved him of any wrongdoing. "And if the fog hadn't been there, you would have seen my car a lot sooner and probably not hit it." She shrugged carelessly. "I don't blame the weatherman, the fog or God. Why should I blame you?"

"Whether or not you blame me is totally irrelevant." The harsh tone momentarily surprised her, but she was becoming used to his gruff manner. It was probably just his way of covering up the fact that he had feelings. "I blame me."

Yes, he did. She could see that. Reaching over, Madison covered his hand with her own. "Are you always so hard on yourself?"

Duncan didn't think he was being particularly hard. It was just the way things were, forged out of practice and experience. Only the best had ever been expected of him. Nothing less was acceptable. Not for a MacNeill. Growing up, he'd hated and chafed against those expectations, but they were now indelibly entered in the book that contained the pages of his life. It was too late to change. Nor did he know how. It was beyond his realm to shirk his responsibility in the matter. Or to ignore it.

In a way, he supposed being raised to demand the peak of perfection from himself was responsible for his very existence now. It kept him alert and on his toes, even more so than the average agent. The life expectancy of an undercover DEA operative was not the sort that compelled life insurance agents to come running in hopes of selling him a policy.

Duncan didn't feel like discussing whether or not he was being hard on himself. "Let's just say I feel I owe you, all right?"

She'd just had another door close in her face, Madison thought. But this door belonged to him, not her. She realized that she was as stubborn as he was.

There was a knock as Madison opened her mouth to protest the thought that he owed her anything at all. "Not all right," she told him firmly. He looked at her in surprise, but she was already turning toward the door.

"Come in," Madison called out, not quite certain who or what to expect. The only person she knew was already here.

She amended that thought as soon as she saw the young nurse enter the room. The woman was pushing a glass bassinet before her.

A bassinet with her son in it, Madison thought. Duncan wasn't the only person she knew. She knew Neil. Feelings flooded her heart, overwhelming it.

"Someone's here to see you," the nurse announced cheerfully. Duncan rose to his feet as she brought the bassinet to a stop at the foot of Madison's bed. "It's feeding time again."

"Already?" Madison tried not to groan. It felt as if she'd stopped feeding Neil only a few minutes before Duncan had come in.

The nurse laughed. "Being a new mother takes a great deal of getting used to. You'll find babies want to eat every four hours, sometimes sooner if they fell asleep during their last feeding." With practiced ease and care, the nurse lifted the infant out of the bassinet. She glanced at Duncan and smiled encouragingly. "Would you like to hold your son before your wife starts feeding him?"

"Oh, he's not my husband," Madison interjected quickly to save him any embarrassment.

"But I would like to hold him." Duncan was already taking the baby from the nurse.

Once he held him in his arms, Duncan felt that same strange, warm response to the infant he'd felt last night. He couldn't begin to analyze it. He didn't even try.

Awake, Neil was waving his tiny fisted hands before his mouth. He tried to suck nourishment from one fist, then the other when the first proved unsatisfying. He switched back again for the same reason. His nose wrinkled, a cry on its way.

Children were not within Duncan's realm of expertise. None of the people who numbered among his small, tight group of friends had any children.

He'd never held an infant before last night. Looking at Neil, he was amazed that people started out so tiny and defenseless and still managed to survive somehow.

"Hold on, little man." Very gently, he drew the fist out of Neil's determined, rosebud mouth. "You're going to suck the skin right off those knuckles if you're not careful."

Madison watched Duncan and her son in utter fascination. A sweet sensation poured through her veins. Duncan's expression had softened the moment the nurse placed Neil in his arms. He almost didn't look like the same man. It was as if she had just witnessed a solid rock turn into a malleable mound of clay. Clay that was being sculpted by a tiny hand.

The nurse closed the door behind her as she left the room. Madison couldn't bring herself to tear her eyes away from Duncan and her son.

"Do you have children of your own?" That would explain a great many things, she thought.

"No. I'm not married," Duncan added as an afterthought, though she hadn't asked. He glanced up, surprised that he had volunteered the information. As a rule, he didn't volunteer anything about himself.

"You don't have to be married to have children." She wasn't, if she was to believe some faceless man she didn't remember meeting.

"Well, I don't have either," he said with finality. "No children, no wife."

"That would explain the baseball and glove." She caught his attention with that. Duncan raised a brow as he looked at her, waiting for an explanation. "It's pretty large for him right now."

"He'll grow into it." Duncan held up his finger

before Neil's face, then slowly began to move it from side to side. It pleased him that the huge green eyes followed his every movement. "Seemed like the thing to get for a boy."

She went for the obvious, hungry for details, any details. "I guess you must have loved baseball as a child."

The laugh was distant, as were his own memories. "I didn't love anything as a child." He'd tried to, when he'd been very young, and had been soundly rebuffed. Neither parent gave or required love where he was concerned. He'd learned that quickly enough.

The statement was chilling as well as telling, Madison realized. "I'm sorry, I didn't mean to pry." She shrugged helplessly when he looked at her. "I guess with nothing of my own to remember, I'm unconsciously trying to tap into your life."

"We'll get you a life," he promised. He made the promise to both mother and child. With no life of her own, how could she give one to her son? "I have a friend on the police force. There's probably a missing person's report out on you."

She wanted to believe that. But reality told her otherwise. "What if there isn't? What if I'm not missing out of anyone's life—I'm just gone?" It was a very real possibility, and now that she said it out loud, it felt likely, even though she couldn't say why.

Neil began to fuss in earnest. It was a sign, Duncan thought. Time for him to go. He handed the baby to Madison.

He'd had the same thought that she had about the missing person's report but saw no reason to say anything until he had something to go on, one way or another.

"No sense in getting ahead of yourself," he warned.

Held against his mother, Neil immediately started rooting at her breast, even though there was a hospital gown in the way. A wet spot began to form on the material just beside his mouth.

Duncan realized he was staring.

"I'd better be going," he told her. "I'm interrupting his lunch." He crossed to the door.

"Will you be back?" Madison began to slide the gown from her shoulder.

It took more effort than he thought to draw his eyes away. He found himself wanting to stay, to remain and quietly watch this most intimate of scenes. It wasn't a feeling he knew he could safely allow to take hold.

"I'll be back," he muttered in reply as he let himself out. He knew he would be, even if she hadn't asked.

Six

"Are you sure you want me to sign this right now, Madison?" Sheila frowned dubiously as she looked at the hospital release form. Signing it was standard procedure, but in Sheila's opinion, Madison was in an undue hurry to leave the hospital. Remaining another day wouldn't hurt the woman any.

Gingerly, Madison stood up. Her legs still felt as if they were just this side of liquefied gelatin, but she knew that would pass. The sooner she got going, the better. A sense of urgency, the source of which she couldn't pinpoint, had been there ever since she'd come to in the car two days ago. It was pushing her now. She couldn't stay here any longer.

"Yes." Madison tried to sound as positive as possible. "I'm sure."

Madison looked more like a waif than a mother, Sheila thought. The maternity dress the woman had had on when she arrived now hung about her body like a recently vacated tent. Sheila was sure she had clothes in her closet that would fit Madison. She'd planned on bringing in a few dresses tomorrow to give her. Madison's request to leave had caught Sheila completely off guard and unprepared. Most new mothers weren't anxious to begin taking care of newborns without a capable set of hands close by. They had a tendency to want to linger in the soothing atmosphere the hospital provided for them as they became acquainted with the newest members of their families.

"I know that most insurance companies try to get you out ten minutes after giving birth," Sheila began gently, "but you can stay longer than two days if you feel you need the extra time." She looked around the room. It was meant for VIPs who could afford to pay for luxury as well as privacy. "We don't exactly have a long waiting list for this maternity suite, and Duncan *is* taking care of the bill."

Madison blew out a breath. That was just the problem. Duncan was taking care of it. She was already far too indebted to the man as it was. She didn't even want to think about what the final tally would come to. Or how she was going to pay it anytime soon.

"Yes, but I *am* going to pay him off eventually and I'd rather not have to contemplate selling my firstborn to do it." And then, because she felt Sheila was really concerned about her well-being, Madison smiled. "Really, I'm fine."

Sheila sorely doubted it. No memory, no last name, no money and a newborn weren't exactly ideal conditions when undertaking anything, much less a new beginning. "Do you have any idea where you'll be going?"

Yes, she had an idea, and it didn't hearten her. But for the time being, there was nothing Madison could do about it. She had to make the best of it.

"The lady from social services gave me a list of shelters where I can go until I find a job." Her smile was self-conscious. Madison dug deep for courage. Finding a scrap, she gathered it to her. Humor followed along naturally. "I don't even know what it is I do, so I guess answering want ads for nuclear physicists is out of the question for the time being.''

Sheila had had experience with shelters. Some were populated with dedicated, caring people who really tried to help. Many others were not. Having taken an instant liking to Madison, she tried to think of an alternate solution. With Slade's family visiting, there was no room at her own house, but maybe there was someplace else where she could temporarily set up Madison and her son until things got straightened out for them.

Her pager began to beep. Shutting it off, Sheila made note of the number. It was her office. She was running behind. Nothing new about that. She slipped her arm around Madison's shoulders. ''Listen, why don't you put off leaving the hospital for a few more hours? Maybe I can arrange something a little nicer for you than a homeless shelter, buy you a little time. Who knows, your memory might suddenly return at any moment—''

''Until it does, you can stay at my house.''

Neither woman had heard Duncan enter the room. They turned almost in unison to look at him.

An audience. He would have preferred saying this to Madison without having anyone else around, even Sheila. But in the long run, he supposed it didn't matter. What mattered to him was doing the right thing, even if it did impose restrictions on his life. The restrictions were only temporary. Just as he hoped Madison's amnesia was.

Duncan had no idea why, but he'd woken up with a hunch that Madison might get it into her head to leave today. The hunch was so strong he'd decided to check on her before he went to the office.

He'd also made up his mind about other things. Like exactly how far his responsibility to this woman went. He saw the surprised look on Sheila's face melt into a smile. She obviously approved of his suggestion. But it wasn't her acquiescence that was necessary. His eyes shifted to Madison.

Her color, he thought, was still far too pale to suit him. Guilt scraped like a sharp-toothed, rusty rake along his conscience.

Madison had thought she'd never see Duncan again. Now that he was here, she knew she would have missed saying goodbye to him. But it seemed that he wasn't interested in saying goodbye just yet. She tried to ignore the tiny kernel of hope that popped open inside her.

"Your house?" she repeated. Was Duncan actually asking her to stay at his home, or had she somehow misheard him?

Madison looked more stunned than afraid. That made two of them, Duncan thought. But he knew that he had no other choice open to him. He could, of course, put her up in a hotel, but he instinctively knew that she would refuse—flatly this time. He couldn't say he'd blame her for that. In her place, he'd do the same.

But this was different. She needed to stay someplace and that place wasn't a shelter. Things happened in shelters. He'd heard enough stories to know. She would be depersonalized and that was the last thing she needed right now.

What Madison needed was to find herself in every sense of the word, and he intended to help. Otherwise, he'd have no peace.

"It's large," he said matter-of-factly, as if people

stayed with him all the time instead of the exact opposite, "and you and Neil will have your own rooms. I'm out most of the time so I won't be getting in your way. I have a housekeeper who comes in twice a week to clean. Rosalie." He deliberately ignored Sheila as he spoke. Ignored, too, the bemused expression on her face. She was looking at him as if he were Saint George, returning from a dragonfest. He wasn't anything of the sort and they both knew that. "I've already called Rosalie and asked her to change her schedule. She'll be coming on full-time for a while to help you with the baby."

Just like that. The man certainly was full of surprises. For a moment, because it would make everything so easy, Madison was tempted. But just because it was easy didn't mean it was right. She shook her head. "I can't accept."

Now that he had made up his mind, Duncan didn't feel like being drawn into a debate. His eyes narrowed, framed with impatience. "Why not?"

"Because…" Unable to stand any longer, Madison abandoned bravado and sank down on the bed, grateful to be off her feet. "Because you're a stranger."

There was a great deal more to it than that, things she couldn't quite put into words, feelings she didn't yet understand herself. What she offered him was the simplest excuse. It was also the only thing she could come up with on short notice.

He dismissed the protest immediately. "Right now, everyone's a stranger to you, so that excuse is ridiculous." His tone challenged her to come up with something else, his eyes forbade it.

Something about this woman had touched him,

Sheila thought, fascinated by the revelation. She'd always believed that Duncan had a soul but until today, she hadn't seen any tangible evidence of it. She did now.

Coming between them, she told Madison, "I can vouch for him," although she really doubted that Madison was personally apprehensive about staying with Duncan. There was something about the man that made you feel infinitely safe without his having to say a single word.

Duncan spared Sheila a cryptic glance. "You have no idea how happy that makes me." His attention shifted back to Madison. "The way I see it, you have no choice. Either you stay at my house or Neil starts his life in a place people turn to as a last resort."

Madison hated the way that sounded. It was hard enough going through with this without having Duncan point out the obvious. "I already told you, I don't blame you for the accident."

"And I told you that what you feel doesn't matter. I have to do what I feel is right." His eyes held hers. "I can't make you come with me, but if you intend to try to pull your life together, you'll stand a better chance of doing it in an atmosphere where your son is well taken care of and you don't have to worry about trying to survive from day to day."

Duncan was making sense, Sheila realized. He was also the perfect solution, although she knew she wouldn't have thought of him herself. "Think of him as your slightly oversize fairy godmother," she told Madison.

Now, there was an image he could do without. Duncan's glance was frosty when he looked at Sheila. "Don't you have somewhere to be?"

"Nowhere as entertaining as here, but—" Sheila sighed as her pager went off again "—you're right. I do have other patients to see. They're probably lining up three-deep by now." Though she guessed that only a few years separated them, Madison brought out her maternal instincts. "Let me warn you, Madison, he has a very annoying habit of being right most of the time. What he isn't," she added, pretending to confide in the other woman, "is quite human. If you ask me, he could do well with having you and Neil around. You'd be doing him a favor. Maybe you can find a way to humanize him."

Duncan shoved his hands into his pockets, biting off a choice comment. Since when had Sheila appointed herself guardian at large?

"Sheila." There was a warning note in his voice.

Sheila stopped only to give his cheek a quick kiss. Raising her hands in surrender, she announced, "I'm gone. Oh, by the way—" she looked at Madison "—I've got a few things that might be just your size. I'll have my housekeeper drop them by your place," she told Duncan just before she hurried out the door.

He waited until the door closed. When it did, he turned to look expectantly at Madison. "So, what'll it be?"

Sheila was right, and the truth of it was, Madison thought, she was relieved to have an alternative to the shelters.

Better the devil you know than the devil you don't know. Where had that come from? she wondered, startled. Was it something someone had once said to her? She wanted desperately to pursue it, but the familiar feeling the phrase generated was already fading. Maybe it would come to her later.

Later.

The very word had a haunting ring to it. But there was *now* to face. And Duncan.

Madison picked her way through the verbal mine-field carefully. "If I say yes, I'm going to wind up being in debt to you forever."

The smile on her face told him all he needed to know. The debate was over. "No, you won't," he said simply. "I don't charge rent."

That wasn't the kind of debt she meant. She had a feeling he knew that. Knew and didn't want to discuss it. But they would, she promised herself. Someday.

Madison stared out the window, fascinated by the view as Duncan drove his car up the winding hill. It was breathtaking. Maybe Sheila had been right. Maybe he was her fairy godmother. It certainly felt as if she were in a fairy tale.

One look at the house at the end of the long drive-way confirmed it. A three-story structure fashioned out of stone that gleamed blue gray in the morning sun, it looked more like a castle than a house in Southern California.

Madison caught her breath as Duncan brought the car to a stop. "You live here?"

Rosalie's black hatchback was parked slightly sideways in the driveway. Good, she'd arrived. Duncan hadn't relished leaving Madison alone, and wait-ing with her until the housekeeper arrived would have made things difficult for him. Rounding the hood, he opened the rear passenger door for Madi-son, then took her arm and helped her out. "Yes."

Madison unbuckled Neil from the tiny baby seat

Duncan had purchased at the gift shop before leaving the hospital. She lifted her son out and stepped away from the car to look at the house again. Towering and majestic in appearance, the building was almost intimidating. A little like the man who owned it.

"Alone?" she asked him.

He looked at her, aware that the invitation he'd extended to Madison and her son was open-ended. "Not anymore."

That hadn't been her question. "I mean, when you aren't taking in people you've run into—no disrespect intended."

"None taken," he answered easily, then added, "Yes, I live alone. When I live here."

She wasn't sure what he meant by that. Did he have two houses? Why would he want another house if he had this one? If it was hers, she'd never look at another house. She might not even want to leave the grounds.

"It's beautiful," she whispered.

Duncan stood back for a moment, trying to see the house from her perspective.

Beautiful. The word more aptly described a woman than a building. He supposed that in the absolute sense, the house was beautiful, although for him the beauty was more than slightly tarnished.

He'd moved back into the house two and a half years ago after his parents had died and left it to him. At the time, it had been the most convenient thing to do. As far as proximity went, this house was better situated than the one he'd lived in previously. It was not only closer to the building where he occasionally reported, but close to his uncle's home and Mac-Neill's Sweets headquarters. Though he left everything up to Thomas as far as running the company went, there were times when his signature as a major stockholder was necessary.

Maybe down deep, it was all an excuse to return to his roots and search for some order to his life. He wasn't sure and hadn't found the time to analyze his motives. For a while, when he'd first moved back, it had been awkward, acclimating himself to a place that had never really been a home to him. A place he'd been in a hurry to leave.

It still wasn't a home. He doubted that it ever would be, not with all the ghosts hovering in the corners. But now, it was what he was used to. One place was more or less like another, he supposed. Moving had even less appeal to him than staying.

"Four walls and a roof," he acknowledged flippantly. Taking out the baby seat for her, he slammed the car door shut with his hip.

How could he say that? Even without memories to fall back on, Madison knew this had to be the most beautiful house she'd ever seen.

"A one-room shack is four walls and a roof. This is a palace. When you invited me, I had no idea your house would be so huge." Stroking Neil's back as she held the infant against her, she looked over her shoulder at Duncan. "No wonder you're lonely."

Defenses he'd hardly been aware of sprang up, immediately locking into position. "Who said I was lonely? Sheila?" It was the only logical guess. But it was the wrong one.

"No, nobody said it, at least not to me." She cocked her head, looking at him. Neil stirred against her. "But you are. It's in your eyes."

The hell it was. Duncan prided himself on keeping

his emotions tightly under wraps and his thoughts from registering on his face. That included his eyes. At times, it had meant his life.

"Don't let your imagination run away with you." He led the way to the front door. "I'm not lonely, and what you see in my eyes is the dread of facing another day of deadly boredom."

It had been less than a month since he'd been placed behind a desk, but he felt as if the adrenaline had been siphoned out of his body and out of his life. Granted, he was busy preparing reports and evidence for the grand jury hearing, which had yet to be scheduled, but that was hardly in the same league as what he'd been doing before. He didn't know how much longer he could put up with strictly cerebral activity. There had to be a way to get back into the field in some capacity as soon as this all died down and the media found something else to focus on.

Being declared World's Most Eligible Bachelor of the month didn't exactly help his cause any, he thought, annoyed.

Duncan took out his keys. It was then that he realized Madison hadn't followed him. Turning, he saw that she was standing where he'd left her, looking toward the back of the house. Now what?

"Are you coming?"

Madison combed her free hand through her hair, trying to hold it in place. The breeze up here was strong. She wondered if it was always like this. Nature airing out its surroundings. "Would it be all right if I went into the backyard?"

The request made no sense. He figured she'd be tired out by the ride and would want to be shown to her room as soon as possible. "Now?"

If she noticed the irritated note in his voice, she gave no indication. "I'd like to see if the view is as spectacular as I think it is."

What difference did that make? Duncan shrugged. The woman was obviously not predictable. "It's a view," was all he said. Seeing that she was serious, he set the baby seat down on the front steps and made his way around the side of the house. Pushing open the back gate, he gestured for her to enter. "After you."

Madison smiled her thanks. As she passed him, the wind whipped her hair against his cheek, trailing the ends along his throat. He stiffened before the action consciously registered. Something dark and secretive rippled through his belly, tightening the muscles. He shook it off, but not as easily as he would have liked.

Madison pulled the cotton blanket over Neil's head to shield the infant from the breeze. It was even stronger back here because there was no building to act as a buffer. The house stood on top of the hill looking down at the city below like a reigning monarch deigning to look down at his subjects. Madison turned slowly, absorbing everything. Colored pavers dovetailed in a brilliant blue-gray-pink pattern all around the perimeter of the house. There was a gazebo perched elegantly in the center of the manicured lawn. Planters completed the picture, bordering the extended patio. A black wrought-iron fence ran the length of the property, stopping just at the point where the hill sloped downward. But what capped it all was the view.

The man knew how to live, Madison thought with deep appreciation. Turning to look at Duncan, she had a feeling that he didn't see what she saw. All this was something that he probably took for granted, something that was just there without his conscious acknowledgment. What was it like to be so complacent about something so magnificent? She hoped that she would never learn.

"It's like standing on top of the world," she told him. Just being here left her breathless. "This must be an incredible sight at night."

With very little effort, she could envision it. The lights of the homes spread out below, shining like so many scattered stars beneath her feet. No wonder he seemed so lofty, so detached. It would be hard not to, if this was what he woke to every morning and what he saw every night before he fell asleep.

"I wouldn't know." He didn't make it a practice to come out here at night. Thinking back, Duncan wasn't sure he ever had, even as a child. There was no attraction here for him, no desire to steep himself in something he considered his parents' house.

He found himself far more taken with the look on Madison's face than any view the hillside house might have to offer. She looked as if she'd been put under a spell, like some enchanted princess.

Enchanted princesses didn't run around with twelve hundred dollars in cash on them, he reminded himself. There had to be more to her than what he saw.

"Don't you come out here to look at it?" She would in his place. Every evening.

"No. Like I said, I'm usually not home." During the two years he'd been undercover, he'd returned to the house less than a handful of times. The bills that came with running it were all handled by his accountant. He saw the house as just another responsibility. It had no other claim on him.

Her smile was warm, inviting when she turned toward him. "How about tonight?"

He didn't follow her. "Tonight?"

The baby started to whimper. Holding him closer, Madison began to rock ever so slightly. The whimpering stopped. The rhythm seemed to soothe Neil. She had a knack for it, Duncan thought.

"Will you be home?" she asked.

He hadn't really planned on it, but there was nothing pressing to keep him at the office, either. In general, other than a scheduled press conference, the department wanted him to maintain a low profile for the time being and they got no argument from him. The lower the better, as far as he was concerned.

"I could be," he allowed cautiously.

"Then it's a date."

The smile curving her generous mouth, moving up like a wisp of curling smoke into her eyes, held his attention a little longer than he was comfortable with.

"A date?"

If Madison didn't know any better, she would have said he looked as if he expected her to unwrap a bomb and set it at his feet. She nodded. "I'll meet you out on the patio at dusk."

He still wasn't getting it. "To do what?"

"Look at the view."

They were doing that now. Why did she want to put an official time to it? He brushed back another strand of her hair as it insisted on playing tag with his face.

"Whatever. Come inside, I want you to meet Rosalie. My housekeeper," he added in case she'd forgotten. "By the way," he remembered, "I've had your car towed to my mechanic's place. It's being repaired. I'll have it driven over when it's ready."

He said it so offhandedly, as if he didn't acknowledge that this was yet another good deed he'd done for her. He really was a very unique man, Madison thought. "Thank you," she murmured.

Duncan didn't bother answering.

Rosalie Salinas had worked for the Stewart MacNeills for the last thirty years. She'd begun as a maid when Duncan was a little boy and had advanced slowly. By the time his parents had died, she'd been the housekeeper for ten years. After living alone, Duncan didn't welcome the idea of having live-in help, so he'd kept her on in a diminished capacity. Rosalie had supplemented her income by working for his uncle, as well.

In her late fifties, she wore sensible shoes and a no-nonsense expression on her face as if they were both standard issue required by her work. Duncan MacNeill paid her a very good salary and she'd never had cause to complain. Surprisingly generous given his uncommunicative nature, he was also a fair man. In the end, that was better than generosity. To be treated fairly was all she asked for.

Which was why, when he had called at a little after seven this morning to ask her to come back to work for him on a full-time basis, she hadn't hesitated. He'd informed her that it would only be for a short while, but she'd secretly hoped it would be permanent.

In comparison to working for his parents, caring for Duncan MacNeill's house was an easy matter.

There was never anything to straighten out, no wild parties to pick up after. For a man, she found him incredibly neat and orderly. It helped that he was rarely there.

She'd grown accustomed to coming in and doing her job undisturbed. Having someone else in the house would change that. She couldn't help wondering just how much of a change she faced.

Rosalie was studying Madison intently. Her expression gave no indication what she thought of the dress Madison was wearing, but Madison could guess. It bothered her that the housekeeper probably thought she was being taken in as an act of charity.

But you are, she told herself. What else could it be?

Madison swore to herself that no matter what it took, she was going to pay Duncan back. Every cent.

Duncan glanced at his watch. Even if he made good time getting to the office, he was still going to be late. Having gotten the introductions out of the way the moment he'd walked in, Duncan wanted to be on his way.

"Rosalie, Madison is new at—" He paused, wondering how much he should tell the woman.

"Everything," Madison supplied. "I'm new at everything." When Rosalie looked at her quizzically, Madison said, "I have amnesia."

Rosalie's expression was stony, her eyes doubtful. Her sharp, dark gaze swept over Madison quickly. "You look all right."

"Amnesia doesn't change the way a person looks, Rosalie." Duncan wasn't accustomed to Rosalie being contrary.

"Of course," she murmured, politely backing off.

She knew how Duncan felt about any attempts at familiarity. Rosalie maintained a respectful distance between them at all times. It worked better for her that way, too. She knew what was expected of her.

"So you can see that I'm going to need a lot of help," Madison told her, deciding to make an ally out of the woman. "But I'll try not to get in your way."

The eyebrow Rosalie raised at the promise was etched with surprise. Her glance shifted to Duncan.

He was more amused than annoyed. "That's not how it works," he told Madison.

Still rocking Neil, Madison looked at Duncan, confused. "There are rules?"

"Between housekeeper and guests, yes." He had to be going. He had another debriefing on the drug bust scheduled. It was the last one, Stringburne had promised him, although he wasn't sure he believed the captain. "I don't have time for this right now, I'm running late. You two work this out between you, okay? If you need anything," he told Madison, "just ask. Rosalie, there'll be a bonus with your check this week for this."

"Very good, Mr. MacNeill." She turned toward her new charge, prepared to have a very long day ahead of her. She wasn't smiling.

As the front door closed, leaving the two women alone with each other, the baby began to cry.

Madison knew exactly how he felt.

she knew how Duncan felt, who'd once struggled to
straighten his life out, been thrown a lifeline of sorts,
bounced around for awhile. It would matter to her.

So how *did* he know what was expected of him?
To use his own experience and attempt to reach a lot of
tough, jaded teenagers in order to make a difference
in the world—that is, to *try* not to get in quite as
big a mess as he had himself, or—

Seven

Duncan's first stop when he left his house wasn't
the building where the DEA had made its offices in
Orange County. Instead, he drove to the Bedford police station. Familiar with the two-story building's
layout, he went directly to the detectives' squad
room. There was someone there he needed to see.

Not wanting to waste time he didn't have, Duncan
called ahead on his cell phone to make sure the man
was on the premises. He made another call, this time
to his own office to inform Stringburne that he would
be later than he'd originally anticipated. The secre-
tary intercepting the call said the captain wouldn't be
pleased. Duncan already knew that.

His life was not as linear as he would have liked.
It never had been, but running into Madison had
made things particularly difficult to juggle. Duncan
was flying by the seat of his pants, his only fuel
coming from his instincts. He had to follow them.

The detectives' squad room looked fairly busy, but
it was an entirely different sort of busy from what
Duncan was accustomed to. The atmosphere here
was different. Even the criminals in Bedford were
upscale. There were no lowlifes, no drug addicts nodding out, slumped in chairs and being guarded while
waiting to give incoherent statements. No gaggle of
prostitutes being herded in, shouting obscenities at

anyone within earshot. There was none of that sweaty desperation that had come to be such a part of the peripheral edges of his life. Everything here was pristine and neat, as if dirt could only be relegated to the lower social ladder.

His mouth curved just a little. His mother, had she been alive, would have still disapproved, seeing the men and women here as "riffraff." She would have been referring to the people on the right side of the law, not the criminals. He wondered if anyone in the real world actually used the word anymore.

Looking around, Duncan saw the object of his impromptu visit sitting at his desk, equal piles of paperwork on either side of his propped-up elbows. There were two buttons undone at the man's collar and his tie was askew. Same old Kelly, he thought.

Frank Kelly looked up as if he sensed rather than heard Duncan approach. At fifty-one, carrying about twenty pounds more than his doctor was happy about, Frank Kelly still looked boyish as he grinned at Duncan.

He tossed aside the report he was working on, appearing glad for the diversion. "Hey, MacNeill, how's your love life?"

For a split second, the question took Duncan aback. He thought Kelly was referring to the woman he'd just left behind at his house. And then he realized that the question and accompanying attempt at a wicked look were aimed at the damned *Prominence Magazine* article.

Duncan had no idea why he'd even thought of Madison in connection with the question. Stupid, he upbraided himself. The look in his eyes was dark as he warned the older man, "Don't start."

Kelly spread his large, capable hands wide in innocent protest. "Me, I'm not starting anything." The laugh was deep and purely at Duncan's expense. "I just thought, after being written up as one of the World's Most Eligible Bachelors on top of all that publicity you got having your mug plastered all over the front page, you'd be beating the ladies off with a stick."

He scrubbed his chin thoughtfully, eyeing Duncan. They had a history, he and Duncan, that went back some seventeen years or so. At the time, Duncan had been the rich kid, caught shoplifting for kicks. Kelly had taken him in hand and shown him just where "kicks" could land him. On the wrong side of iron bars. The lesson had stuck admirably. Kelly figured it gave him the right to hassle the younger man from time to time. It was all in fun. When push came to shove, Kelly knew that there wasn't a man better at his job than Duncan. He took a little credit for that himself.

"Got any overflow for a poor neglected police detective?" he wanted to know.

A vague smile flirted with Duncan's mouth. As if Kelly needed any more women in his life. "What, so you can get a third divorce?"

It was no secret that Kelly maintained fairly decent relationships with his two ex-wives. There were no kids involved, but there were three dogs and he had visiting rights to them. Despite being a two-time loser matrimonially, Kelly was an incurable optimist where the fairer sex was involved. He and Duncan, Kelly knew, were on opposite sides of the coin when it came to that.

"You cut right to the pessimistic view, don't you,

boy? No shortcuts for you." Kelly shook his head sadly, only half kidding. "Haven't you ever heard that third time's the charm?"

The look on Duncan's face said that he'd heard of it. It also said what he thought of the phrase. "Just a superstition," Duncan declared.

Scooting away from his desk, Kelly leaned back in his chair to reach a bookcase directly behind him. It was made out of wood rather than metal. He rapped on it three times, only partially for effect. "Hey, superstitions are my life." He eyed Duncan closely, the curious cop in him taking over. "So, Agent MacNeill, what can I do you for?"

Duncan placed a hand on top of the computer monitor on Kelly's desk. "I want you to go through your missing person's database."

Kelly moved his chair back in front of his desk, interested. "Why, you missing someone?"

"No, I found someone."

There was almost a pregnant note in Duncan's voice. Kelly waited for details and told himself he should have known better. Duncan was a clam. "So, what's the problem?"

Duncan glanced at his watch. Ten thirty-three. The morning was evaporating on him. "She doesn't know who she is."

Studying Duncan's face, Kelly tried to decide if this was on the level. He leaned back in his chair. "Is this before or after you kissed her?"

Duncan blew out a breath, knowing he should have given the details at the start, yet hating the way the admission made him feel. He hadn't been careless or drunk, but that didn't change the fact that he might have unwittingly destroyed the woman's life.

At least as she knew it. "This is after I hit her with my car."

"Oh." So that was it. Duncan's motivation was a crushing sense of responsibility. Typical. "She hurt?"

Duncan shrugged away the question. "Just a bump on the head, but she can't remember who she is and she had nothing on her to identify her."

"Nothing at all?"

"Nothing," Duncan repeated. Then, because every detail was necessary, he added, "Except the baby she gave birth to right after the accident."

The surprised look on Kelly's face was there and gone before it had time to register. "Boy, this just gets better and better." Shaking his head, Kelly centered his keyboard on the desk. "Okay, give me a description and we'll see if we can get a match for you."

There was no match.

Duncan had had a feeling there wouldn't be, but he knew he had to try. There were more than a few descriptions in the database that fit Madison, but they all proved to be dead ends once photographs attached to the files were pulled up. Whoever Madison was, either she hadn't been gone long enough for someone to think filing a report was necessary, or there was no one close enough to her to file one.

A third alternative suggested itself to Duncan as Kelly conducted another sweep through the system, extending the search to include neighboring states. Maybe she wasn't really missing, and her amnesia, for reasons that hadn't come to light yet, was all a hoax. It was a possibility.

Away from Madison, from the softening look in her eyes, Duncan felt suspicions creep in. Nothing, he had learned over the years, could be taken at face value. That included a woman with wide green eyes that seemed capable of looking down into a man's very soul.

"How about this one?" Kelly turned the monitor toward Duncan.

He knew before he looked what the answer would be. Nothing was ever simple or easy. At least, not for him. "No."

"Want to go east?" Kelly moved the mouse to scroll toward the screen that included the Midwestern states.

He'd already wasted time he didn't have. Maybe later, Duncan thought. "No, that's okay. It was a long shot."

Kelly shut down the program. "The best hunches usually are."

"Thanks, anyway." Duncan turned toward the door.

"Call me if you get anything else you need checked out," Kelly called after him.

Duncan merely nodded to acknowledge that he'd heard. Apparently this wasn't something that was going to go away in a matter of a few hours. He'd already had Ed Jackson checked out. The man was exactly who and what he said he was and had no connection to Madison, other than selling her his car.

Duncan now had to face the fact that, unlike most things in his life, this was something that had an indefinite time limit attached to it. Madison, if that was really her name and not just something that had popped into her head, could remember who she was tomorrow. Or a thousand tomorrows from now. And until she did, she was his responsibility.

That had not been drummed into his soul by his parents, both of whom had been very big on the family name only so far as having it remain untarnished, but by his uncle Thomas, who was more interested in living up to a code of ethics than a surname.

Frustration was walking beside Duncan by the time he got off on the third floor of the federal building and strode toward the large communal room where his desk was. The recycled air felt particularly stifling to him.

Even from the vantage point of the threshold, he could see that there was a mountain of papers on his desk. A mountain that hadn't been there when he left late yesterday afternoon. Now what? He took his time reaching it, knowing that whatever the explanation, he wasn't going to like it.

"All right, what is all this?" Duncan looked at the person closest to his desk. A man he had undergone training with at DEA headquarters in Quantico, an event that made the other man feel they had bonded. Bonding, Duncan believed, was the exclusive prerogative of glue designed for such things. Men did not bond. They occasionally had things in common. That was the case between him and Fontana. Especially after Fontana had shown *Prominence Magazine* around, marking off page one hundred and four in case anyone missed the insipid article.

Tony Fontana had a wide mouth that was quick to split into a grin and an annoying habit of not knowing when to stop talking. It was one of the reasons, along with his ability to retain vast amounts of information and keep them straight, that their superiors had elected to keep Tony back behind the lines and at his desk, where he could do the most amount of good and least amount of harm.

Today the grin on Tony's face was wide enough to drive a medium-size moving van through. "Fan mail," he crowed in response.

Duncan glared, his brow forming one dark line across blue eyes that were far from friendly. "I'm in no mood for jokes, Fontana."

Tony was on his feet and beside Duncan's desk in an instant. Danger was not something he recognized when it came in the guise of someone he thought of as a friend. This left him wide-open.

"Tense, are we?" Tony sifted a few letters through his hands, letting them fall back on Duncan's desk. "I'm sure any one of these lovely contestants would love to help you get rid of some of that excess tension." The wink was broad and incredibly annoying, even given the fact that it was coming from Fontana. "If you get my drift."

It had to be a put-on. According to Fontana, the magazine had only been on the stands a couple of days. The man could make a computer all but sit up and beg. This so-called mail had to have come from him, cancellation marks on the stamps and all. Duncan was in no mood to appreciate the effort or the creativity that had gone into this.

"You're going to be drifting in the middle of the ocean," Duncan warned him, "if you don't get rid of this junk."

Fontana laughed. "Is that any way to talk about your adoring public?"

Duncan had a meeting he had to go to at eleven-thirty and there were still some things he wanted to take care of before then. He didn't have time for whatever convoluted game Fontana was playing.

"I don't have an adoring public." He looked at Fontana expectantly.

Fontana made no effort to clear away the letters. "World's Most Eligible Bachelor, the man women would most like to be handcuffed to." He peered at Duncan's face. "Any of this ring a bell?"

What he wanted to ring, or wring, was the man's overly long neck. "More like a death knell."

If you want a thing done... Sweeping the back of his hand across the piles, Duncan sent three stacks flying off his desk. A few letters landed in the waste-paper basket. Most landed around it.

Shaking his head, Fontana bent down and began to pick up the excess. Before the man could put them back on his desk, Duncan ordered, "Leave them there."

Fontana rose, holding two handfuls against his chest. "They've cut back on the cleaning service. We're supposed to police our own area, remember?" He glanced down at the letters. "Besides, if you don't want them, I'll take them. Maybe I'll find the girl of my dreams here."

Nobody was that desperate. "You want a groupie?" Duncan's tone told Tony what he thought of that idea.

Fontana had the body of a pipe cleaner and a face that a mother would be challenged to love. "Hey, as long as she's breathing, it's okay. I'm not fussy."

Duncan waved at the letters. "Then take them all. My compliments."

Fontana gave a cursory glance at some of the return addresses. There was one from Beverly Hills. "Must be nice to be that confident."

"Confidence has nothing to do with it." Duncan unlocked the center drawer. Notes for some of his preliminary reports were stuffed into a folder. Where his own work was concerned, he believed in pen and paper rather than computers. Paper was easier to destroy. "I just don't have the time. Or the inclination."

Fontana's brows rose high, reaching out toward a hairline that was swiftly retreating. "For adoring women? Man, you're even colder than your reputation makes you out to be." As he spoke, Fontana opened a letter at random. "This is a pretty color," he said wryly, indicating the mint-colored envelope. Duncan said nothing. "Maybe I should clear out of here before I wind up with frostbite to parts of me that can't be replaced."

As he glanced at the letter he'd opened, Fontana's grin faded. He reread the first line. "Hey, MacNeill, I think you'd better read this one."

Duncan didn't even look up. "I've got more important things to do than read a letter that came from—"

But Fontana was already placing the letter squarely in front of him. "No, you don't." He jabbed insistently at the eight-by-ten paper with his finger.

Annoyance and impatience receded. Duncan looked down at the letter and read. Written in a common font found on any computer, the letter Fontana had pulled out at random had nothing to do with the article in *Prominence Magazine* and everything to do with the recent drug bust.

In very graphic terms, it described how Duncan

would die for his part in the drug cartel breakup. The images were particularly chilling when it came to warning him about not testifying.

Fontana moved to take the letter back. "We'd better show Stringburne."

Duncan remained seated. He wasn't worried about an assailant who took the trouble to announce his intentions. His concern had always been about the one in the shadows. The one who attacked without warning. "It's an empty threat."

"And what if it's not?" Fontana asked.

Duncan covered the subtle bulge formed by his shoulder holster. "Then it's not as if I were exactly defenseless."

The letter threatened his family, but he didn't have any, other than Thomas. Thomas could take care of himself. Nevertheless, Duncan made a mental note that it wouldn't hurt to tell his uncle to beef up security around his house.

Fontana smacked his forehead with the palm of his hand. "Right, what was I thinking? You'll just use one of the bags of fan mail to block the bullets." He looked at Duncan, exasperated.

If Duncan had reacted to every so-called threat to his life, he would have become completely paralyzed and inoperative years ago. It was a matter of distancing himself from this kind of thing. His eyes were flat as he turned them toward Fontana.

"This goes with the job, you know that."

Fontana refused to back down. "So does caution."

Duncan thought of the risks he'd been forced to take. Risks that could curl an average man's hair. "Since when?"

Fontana played the department's ace card. "Since

without you, the case doesn't exactly fall apart, but it gets damn rickety.'' Taking out a handkerchief, Fontana picked up the pristine piece of paper again. They both knew there would be no fingerprints on it, but they might get lucky with a watermark. ''Now, are you going to tell the captain, or do you want me to do it?''

Sighing, Duncan got up. He took the letter, handkerchief and all, from Fontana. ''I've got to see the captain this morning, anyway. I might as well bring this with me.''

''Don't forget to give me back the handkerchief,'' Fontana called after him.

Duncan said nothing.

Duncan waited for the light to turn green. Was it him, or did the traffic lights take an inordinately long time to change this time of night? He was bone-tired and wanted to get home. The day had been one of those endless, taxing ones where one thing had piled on top of another.

He'd met with several of the DEA's top officials, not to mention the federal prosecutor who would be handling the case if and when it got to trial. The if and when depended on the grand jury. Duncan never placed bets when it came to the way a grand jury thought.

As far as proceedings went, he'd been the keynote player today. An ironic place to be for a man who hated the limelight.

The death threat had thrown even more attention his way. Like a man who had gone on a fifty-mile forced march, all he wanted to do was burrow into some anonymous hole and get out of the glare of the spotlight. Was that too much to ask?

Apparently, he thought with a disgusted sigh.

The light changed and Duncan's mind turned toward Madison as he drove. How had she spent her day? he wondered. How would he have spent it if he couldn't remember what it was he was supposed to be doing? A distant sympathy stirred within him. It had to be hell for her.

Duncan was relieved to see that Rosalie's car was not in the driveway when he pulled up. One less person to deal with. Because of the hour, he assumed that Madison would be in her room, most likely asleep, but in any event out of the way. He wanted solitude. It was his way of unwinding.

The warm scent of something tempting and spicy greeted him the instant he unlocked the door and walked in. He was surprised Rosalie had prepared something for him. That wasn't part of the arrangement. And then he remembered that she would have had to feed Madison. Vaguely, he wondered if there was any left over.

Dormant taste buds stirred, protesting that all he'd had in the last five hours was a gallon of marginal coffee and a sandwich made up of something largely unidentifiable from one of those cafés that were routinely springing up these days. He'd become accustomed to not caring about what he ate. Something, he knew, that would have horrified his parents. Not because meals like the ones he consumed were bad for his health—neither had been concerned with triviality like that, and his father had died of a massive heart attack at fifty-one—but because such meals were so "plebeian," as his mother was fond of saying. She'd never had a sandwich in her life.

He ate like the men he consorted with—on the run. Meals were to be consumed so that the body could continue functioning, nothing more.

But the aroma in the house was so strong it whetted his appetite. Like an enticing siren, it lured him toward the kitchen rather than up the stairs to his room. The dining room was on the way. It was where he stopped his odyssey.

The dining-room table, covered with a lacy white cloth, was set for two. The candles, from the faint scent of sulfur that wafted toward him as he drew closer, had just been lit. Duncan stared at them. He didn't remember there being candles around.

Rosalie probably kept them in case of a power failure, he decided. But what were they doing, flickering in the breeze his approach had created?

"Hi. Are you hungry?"

Surprised to discover he wasn't alone, Duncan turned around without answering.

It was an evening for surprises.

Madison was standing behind him, wearing a simple blue dress instead of the tent he'd left her in.

She realized he was looking at her dress and flushed with pleasure. Wearing it made her feel a little more human.

"Slade, Dr. Pollack's husband, stopped by earlier to bring over some clothing she thought I might like." Madison spread the skirt out with one hand, letting him get a better look. "It fits."

Yes, it certainly did, he thought. Fit rather nicely on a body that was far trimmer than he'd thought it would be. "You look good," he muttered.

The comment made her smile widen. "Thank you. He's very nice. Dr. Pollack's husband," she explained. "They both are."

"Never met him."

"She wants you to," Madison told him. "Slade said he'd like you to come over for dinner this weekend. Dr. Pollack's not on call and she wants to make an evening of it. She invited me, too, but..." Madison shrugged, letting the rest of her sentence trail off.

Duncan refused to get into a discussion about an invitation that came out of left field. Instead, he dismissed it with a noncommittal, "We'll see." The aroma was giving him no peace. "What did she make?"

Madison looked at him blankly. "She?"

"Rosalie." He nodded toward the kitchen. "What did she make?"

Oh, he meant the aroma. Madison had become so used to it she didn't notice it any longer. "Oh, that. That's me."

He looked at her quizzically; she found it difficult to form coherent sentences when he stared at her that way. Everything still felt so jumbled in her head, so disoriented. There were thoughts flying around in there, moving swiftly like whizzing hummingbirds that refused to pause or alight on anything long enough for her to make sense of them.

"I mean, I made that." Pleasure filled her eyes at her own accomplishment. "I thought that the least I could do after all you've done for me was cook dinner."

"You cook?" His expression turned skeptical.

She nodded. Her momentum built as she spoke

and excitement infused her voice. "I just started puttering in the kitchen after I put Neil down for a nap and things began to come to me."

"What things?"

She knew what he was after. She wished she could give him something positive. For both their sakes. "Cooking things. Nothing that would make a difference."

Duncan tried not to notice the way the disappointment in her voice bothered him.

Eight

Duncan looked down at the serving on his plate. This wasn't a meal that had been thrown together haphazardly. Thought had gone into this as well as planning. He knew for a fact that beef Wellington required ingredients that weren't in his kitchen. His refrigerator did little else than occasionally house leftover take-out food and, even less frequently, fruits when he remembered to buy them.

She had put herself out, Duncan thought. He looked up from his plate to see that she was watching him and trying to appear as if she wasn't.

Madison wouldn't have made much of a spy. The thought initially struck him as humorous, then lingered like the ring left on a table by a glass of water on a hot day. Was that on purpose? he wondered.

"You didn't have to do this, you know." He'd actually rather that she hadn't. It made him uncomfortable to know that she had gone out of her way to cook for him. It implied things, put the two of them on a footing he didn't want. Their business together was that he had caused Madison's accident and subsequent memory loss. Somehow, he intended to put that right. Whether it was by finding her family or helping her regain her memory, it didn't matter. He had a debt to pay and he intended to pay it. She wasn't supposed to blur the lines by doing something for him.

"Yes, I did."

The words were softly spoken, but he detected a vein of stubbornness beneath them. His eyes held hers. "No one's keeping tally."

Madison raised her chin a little. Just enough to convince Duncan his assessment about her stubbornness was right on target. "I am."

He was about to tell her that she shouldn't, since he wasn't, but he knew firsthand the futility and the ultimate fate of that argument. She had told him in the hospital not to hold himself responsible for her accident since she didn't, and he'd answered that it didn't matter if she did or not, because he did.

In a way, Duncan supposed that made them even. And maybe a little bit alike. The last thought refused to leave, hanging on like the subtle perfume of a lover the morning after.

Since the food was before him and he was hungry, Duncan ate. And appreciated the meal more with each mouthful that he consumed. He slanted a glance across the table toward Madison. Once he had begun eating, she'd joined in. She had a healthy appetite, he'd give her that. It occurred to him that she must have held off eating herself until he came home. Why? She hadn't a clue what his hours were. He hadn't told her. For all she knew, he could have remained out all night. The woman was becoming more of a puzzle rather than less.

He looked in her direction again and their eyes met. "Shouldn't you be getting some rest?" he suggested. Duncan took a second, smaller helping. He noticed the smile in her eyes. "Neil'll probably be awake again soon."

At least, that's what he assumed. Hadn't Murphy said something about his newborn sleeping no more than three hours at a clip when he'd first come home from the hospital? Duncan figured most infants behaved identically.

Touched by his concern, Madison refused to entertain the thought that perhaps Duncan was merely trying to get rid of her. She'd found herself anticipating his return for the last couple of hours, ever since Rosalie had left.

"He fell asleep just a few minutes before you came home." Madison had already gauged her son's sleeping pattern. Neil popped up like toast every four hours, awake and hungry. "That still gives me an hour or so before he's up again."

Duncan finished what remained on his plate. He debated taking a third helping, then decided he might regret it. "Don't you need to sleep, too?"

"I'm afraid to go to sleep." She'd remained awake ever since Duncan had left her here, despite Rosalie's stern maternal urgings that she take a nap. Duncan looked at her curiously. He probably thought she was crazy.

"Afraid of slipping into a void," she explained. That's what had been waiting for her both nights at the hospital. Big, gaping voids. It was like falling into a bottomless hole. She'd woken up both times feeling almost despondent. "I guess what I'm doing is trying to absorb as much as I can in hopes that one thought'll jostle another until something gets triggered and I remember."

Madison looked at him, hoping that made sense.

She smiled ruefully. He was undoubtedly tired and didn't want to hear this. It sounded too much like complaining and she didn't mean it to. She saw that he had retired his fork. "Did you enjoy it?"

She was fishing and she knew it, but right now, she needed to hear a compliment. Something positive aimed in her direction. It had felt so good, standing in the kitchen and doing things by instinct.

Her question, coming from nowhere, caught him off guard. "What?"

"The meal." She gestured at his plate. "Did you enjoy it?"

"Yes." He looked at his plate absently, his thoughts elsewhere. "It was very good."

She could detect his preoccupation. Little wonder, seeing what he did for a living. "You say that as if you weren't sure." She wanted him to be honest with her. Nothing but honesty, no matter what. She needed it. "It's all right, you can tell me. A man like you is probably used to gourmet meals. If I fell short, it's okay." This time, her smile bordered on mischievous. "After all, I'm just learning." *Everything,* a small voice whispered in her head.

Her smile was even more appealing than her meal was. Very deliberately, Duncan drew his eyes away from her mouth and focused on the choice of words that had caught his attention.

"What do you mean, a man like me? What do you know about me?" He'd told her next to nothing, and in more than twenty years, Rosalie had never run off at the mouth.

The letter he'd received today came to mind. The one that threatened his life. Whoever had sent it had been extremely careful. The paper didn't even have a watermark, much less fingerprints, and it had been mailed right from the federal building. That pointed to someone both intelligent and brazen.

The next thought materialized out of the blue. Once out, it seemed to follow logically. Could what happened the other night on the fog-enshrouded road have been a setup? Could Madison be something other than what she seemed? Could she be a plant by the organization that had backed the drug cartel? He knew that at best the DEA had caught only half the people involved in the massive network.

At face value, the idea seemed impossible, and yet...why not? He'd be on the lookout for the conventional, a chance meeting with a beautiful woman under normal circumstances. He wouldn't be on his guard when it came to a dazed pregnant woman with amnesia, not by any stretch of the imagination. Which was the beauty of the plan.

He couldn't help wondering if he was being unduly paranoid or shrewd.

"I don't know very much," she admitted. "But I saw you on the news. Rosalie thought it might be a good idea for me to watch television, see if anything looked familiar." She had channel surfed until a still photograph of Duncan, followed by a film clip of a news conference earlier in the week, had stopped her. Madison leaned into him as a growing enthusiasm underlined her words. "The all-news channel had a five-minute story on you and the drug bust you just spearheaded." Clearly impressed, she looked at Duncan with admiration in her eyes. He almost squirmed. "You know, you lead a very dangerous life."

The newscaster, a perfectly made-up redhead, had taken great glee in mentioning that fact and embellishing it. The very thought had Madison shivering, although Rosalie had scarcely paid attention when Madison had called her over to watch. To the housekeeper it was all old news.

Duncan shrugged. He operated by carefully planning for as many contingencies as he could conceive, then forging ahead without worrying about the danger involved. Anything else would only have gotten in his way and tripped him up. "It's a life."

That wouldn't be the way she'd describe it, Madison thought. And it hadn't been the way the newscaster had described it, either. The woman had made it sound as if Duncan were the American answer to James Bond. Madison shifted in her chair, fascinated. What made a man like Duncan, a man who had everything, according to the story, risk his life like that? Was it a sense of honor, a nobleness or something else?

"Is that why you're so tense all the time?"

Maybe it was time to call it a night. Duncan rose, taking his plate with him. He'd put in too long a day to answer any more of her questions. Even if he was given to sharing his thoughts, he had entirely too many questions of his own buzzing in his brain.

Depositing his empty plate into the dishwasher, he swiftly began reviewing the events of the last few days, looking for a clue to validate the uneasy suspicions that had sprung up about Madison.

Madison was aware that he had made no answer. She thought it was because he felt uncomfortable talking about himself.

"Because if you are," she said as she followed him into the kitchen, "you really should learn to relax."

He wasn't about to take advice dispensed by someone who didn't even know her last name. Or so she said. Besides, for him, not being relaxed was a plus. "Tension keeps me alert."

She could see why he'd need that. She could also see why it might be detrimental. "There's such a thing as being too tense, too alert. When you overwind an alarm clock, the spring breaks."

Duncan slammed the dishwasher door abruptly and turned around to look at her, an odd expression on his face. Had she said something wrong?

"What?"

"People don't wind up clocks anymore," he told her. "That was something they did fifteen years ago or so. Before digital timepieces took over the market."

He studied her face. Was that a deliberate slip, or was something beginning to come back to her? It was hard to gauge, not knowing exactly what he was up against. He wouldn't have this problem, he supposed, if he had listened to Thomas and his father and gone into the family business. It certainly would have made life simpler.

And duller.

The implication behind Duncan's words stopped Madison in her tracks. Her face lit up like a Fourth of July sparkler raised high against the dark night. The excitement in her eyes was pure and intense.

She grabbed hold of his arm. "Do you think I'm remembering something from my past?"

It took effort not to get caught up in the look in her eyes, in her enthusiasm. He wondered if that was the way she had looked up at her lover the night she conceived her son.

"Could be," he allowed guardedly. And then again, he thought, this *could* all be an act. An elaborate act to get at him when he least expected it. It might seem far-fetched, but it was no more far-fetched than spending two years of his life setting up the perfect trap to save from ruin the lives of people he would never meet, would never recognize if he passed them on the street. He lived with the far-fetched every day. Why not this?

Madison could feel his eyes on her, could feel something very uneasy, very nervous responding within her. She couldn't put an exact name to the feeling, but it was a nervousness she could grow to like.

She wasn't conscious of running the tip of her tongue along her lips.

Duncan tried not to be.

She cocked her head. "Why are you looking at me like that?"

He took a step away from her, finding he needed the space. "Like what?"

She was trying desperately to understand this world she found herself in. That included understanding him. "Like you're trying to decide what I am."

The fact that she sensed his doubt increased his uneasiness. If she was a plant...

Duncan decided to launch a counterattack of his own. With less effort than he thought it would take, he slipped into the persona he'd so recently abandoned once the drug bust had gone down. He became the slightly cynical, slightly devil-may-care, amiable womanizer who had charmed, oiled and conspired his way into gaining a key position within Carlos Montoya's organization. The space he'd acquired a moment ago was forfeited. He moved closer to her. "Maybe I'm noticing what a beautiful woman you are."

For half a heartbeat, the breath caught in her throat. And then she realized he was teasing her. "Then you *are* tired."

She said it so guilelessly either she was the world's best actress or she meant it, Duncan thought. He almost found himself leaning toward the latter. Didn't she think she was attractive? Beautiful, he amended. Rested, with her long blond hair swaying over her shoulder and in a dress that fit her body so well he would have sworn she couldn't have given birth only two short days ago, Madison was a great deal more attractive than the dazed, exhausted woman he had first encountered on the hillside.

Maybe that was the idea.

Madison suddenly took his hand. "Come outside," she coaxed. She'd wanted to do this ever since she had walked into the backyard this morning. "Maybe the view will relax you."

Duncan doubted very much that anything would relax him. Certainly not standing beside her. And not just because he had suddenly become aware of how lovely a creature she was. That was only a small part of it. The rest, he knew, would be there to taunt him until he discovered who she really was. Until then, he'd be on his guard.

Resigned to yet another night of sleeping with one eye open, Duncan allowed himself to be led outside. He tried not to be aware of how small Madison's hand felt, wrapped around his. Or how nice.

What he concentrated on was the thought that maybe playing along with her would give him further insight into this woman who claimed not to know herself. Help him tip the scales one way or another. It was worth a shot.

Glancing behind her, Madison was satisfied to see that the kitchen window was open. She would hear the baby monitor if she needed to.

Pleased that Duncan acquiesced so readily, she looked up at him as she came to the wrought-iron fence that looked down over the edge of the hill. He wasn't all that tall, but it felt as if he were. There was a presence to him that seemed to tower over her, that made her feel safe even when she might very well not be.

"Now, take a deep breath," she instructed, "and hold it." She did the same, her eyes fluttering shut briefly. Somehow, it made everything seem more vivid that way. "Okay, now let it out slowly."

What was she up to? "Lamaze classes?" he asked, almost amused.

She looked confused at the question, then shook her head. "No, something that just came to me. Is that Lamaze?"

No one was that innocent, and yet on her, it was almost believable. For the time being, he had no choice but to let it ride. "So they say. I don't have any firsthand knowledge," he reminded her.

That's right, no wife, no children. He was alone. Like she was right now. It made her feel closer to him.

"I just thought it might help you with your tension. That and looking up at the stars. They are beautiful, aren't they?" She almost whispered the question, as if being out here like this were like being allowed to tread on sacred ground.

What would help him with his tension was not having the news media hound him. Or not having to take center stage at the grand jury.

Or not having her in the house.

The last had come out of nowhere. He attributed it to his suspicions about her identity. With practiced care, he blocked his thoughts, keeping them from encroaching on his face. Instead, he laughed. "That's a lot to ask of a single breath."

"That's how it all starts." She thought of her son. Neil hadn't cried when he was born, yet he was alive and thriving. "With a single breath. One after another."

Closing her eyes, Madison took another deep breath, then exhaled very slowly. Her head fell back just a little as a tiny dollop of peace trickled through her veins. It was a beginning, she thought.

When she opened her eyes, she found she was looking directly into Duncan's. Even in the dim light from the house, his eyes looked to be an incredible shade of blue. A warm, liquid blue. Like the ocean on a summer's day.

"You're not breathing," she pointed out. At least, not the way she'd told him to.

"Yes," he replied very quietly, "I am."

And what he was also doing, he realized, was watching her. Studying her. Absorbing her. The result was almost hypnotic. And not at all what he was after.

Something stirred within Madison. Something urgent and basic. A half that reached out to a whole. The need that slammed into her, unannounced, was so great she could hardly bear it. Her heart began hammering hard. Madison tilted her face upward. "Duncan?"

He'd never heard his name uttered like a prayer before. Duncan wasn't sure he could have looked away if he wanted to. "Yes?"

Madison didn't know where her courage came from, or even if courage was normally a factor in her life. All she knew was she heard herself saying, "If you wanted to kiss me, it's all right."

The softly voiced assurance vibrated right through him. It was on the tip of his tongue to deny the desire, but he discovered that he couldn't. Not if he was being truthful, at least with himself.

The desire was there.

She had recognized it before he had. Rather insightful, he thought, drawing on cynicism as if his life depended on it, for a woman who claimed not to know anything.

Testing the ground he was entering, Duncan skimmed the tips of his fingers along the slender column of her neck. It filled him with a strange sort of wonder to feel her tremble in response. Tremble, but not move.

Curious, drawn, he lowered his mouth until it hovered hardly an inch over hers. He expected her to take it from there.

She didn't play it the way he expected.

Instead, she waited, her eyes already drifting shut in anticipation of something she sensed she wasn't fully prepared for.

The smart thing to do, Duncan thought, would be to draw away and see what her next move would be. Doing the smart thing was the way he'd survived. It was what he'd done all along. Except this time.

This time, he followed instincts that came from an entirely different source than the one he usually tapped into. Instincts that he commonly ignored. Instincts that refused to be ignored. Bringing his mouth down to hers, Duncan kissed Madison.

At first the kiss was light, as if he were sampling a drink he'd never encountered before. One taste begged for another, a deeper one. And then another. Very quickly, there was a loosening of the control that was as much a part of him as his hands or his legs. As much a part of him as breathing. Duncan deepened the kiss, not from curiosity but because he wanted to. Needed to. Because he couldn't help himself.

It was like swimming up from the bottom of the pool, waiting to break the surface and catch his breath. He couldn't do it, couldn't catch his breath. Someone had moved the surface. It was a lot farther off than he remembered.

He felt the rush come over him, a rush he couldn't shake. He didn't want to. His hand slipped from Madison's face, down along her shoulder until it came to rest at her back. He pressed her to him, feeling his pulse race. Feeling other things, as well. Things that were vague and unclear, hovering on the recesses of his consciousness like a muted Greek chorus standing off in the distance.

A noise, small and muffled, wedged its way into his consciousness just as he broke the surface. Duncan drew back, wondering if he'd actually heard something or if it was only his imagination. He was already blaming his imagination for the reaction he'd just thought he experienced.

Because she didn't remember anything beyond the

framework of the last two days, Madison felt as if she had been kissed for the first time. And what a first time. Duncan made her very blood sizzle. Even now, as he drew away, she was having trouble focusing. It was difficult to orient herself to her surroundings when the top of her head was threatening to come off. The night had suddenly turned balmy, and she squelched the desire to fan herself.

Madison looked at Duncan, her eyes almost as dazed as they had been when he'd first approached her at the scene of the accident. But this time, he noted, the dazed look was one of wonder. And pleasure.

Why did that please him so much? There was no reason for him to be pleased. He was no further along in deciding whether or not she was on the level. If anything, the kiss had muddled things even more.

"You're not relaxed yet."

Was it his imagination, or did she look a little smug when she said that?

"That was definitely not relaxing," he told her. If anything, it had heightened his tension until he felt like a taut bow with no arrow to set free. He wasn't accustomed to reacting that intensely to a woman. Companionship had never been very high on his list of priorities. His way of life did not encourage relationships, and if he thought about it at all, he felt it was unfair to subject a woman to living with the dangers his life revolved around. But what he'd said to Kelly was true. He rarely thought about it. He was fine just the way he was. Alone.

He heard the noise again. It was louder this time. A kitten mewling? Duncan looked around for the source. With the house located so high up on the hill, it wasn't uncommon to have wildlife slink along the perimeters, venturing out in the night for food.

"What is that?" he muttered under his breath.

"Neil," Madison said, suddenly realizing the source of the sound. She upbraided herself for getting so involved with her own feelings that she hadn't heard her son crying. There was no excuse for that. Withdrawing from Duncan, she was already crossing to the double french doors. "He's calling room service for his late-night snack."

How could they hear him out here? Duncan glanced toward the open kitchen window.

"Rosalie put a baby monitor in the kitchen. She said it belonged to one of her daughters," Madison called over her shoulder as she disappeared into the house.

He stared after her. Rosalie had daughters? How had Madison managed, in less than a day, to discover more about the woman than he had in all these years? Who *was* this woman who had just disrupted his pulse rate?

Nine

"Burning the midnight oil?"

Ric Stringburne, Duncan's direct superior and head of the division, looked at Duncan in surprise as he let himself out of his glass-enclosed office. Stringburne thought he was the last one left on the floor. A widower with only a cat in his apartment that might or might not be waiting for him, Stringburne habitually arrived early and remained late. He stopped next to Duncan's desk. "You've already impressed everyone who counts in the department. What are you doing here this late?"

Duncan glanced up briefly. "Just finishing up a few things, Captain." They were things that could very well have waited until tomorrow, but Duncan hadn't wanted to go home until late.

Stringburne nodded. "Very commendable." He knew there were probably other reasons, but he didn't press. The secret to working here was knowing when to push and when to let things pass. He began walking out. "Get home before you wind up finishing yourself up. Oh—" he paused for a moment, looking at Duncan "—and watch your back when you leave. We want to keep it intact until this whole thing is put to rest."

Touching, Duncan thought. "Don't worry."

"That's what they pay me for." Stringburne's

voice echoed back from the hallway as he walked to
the bank of elevators.

Duncan put down his pen and stretched. Stringburne was right. It was time he was getting home.
Madison had to be asleep by now.

Shutting off his computer, Duncan rose. He'd
called earlier this afternoon and spoken to Rosalie,
asking her to stay the night because he wouldn't be
home until very late.

The sound of his footsteps was swallowed up by
the newly installed carpet as Duncan walked to the
elevators a few minutes later. He'd asked Rosalie to
remain because no matter who Madison was, he
didn't care for the idea of leaving her and Neil alone
in the large house. If he was wrong about the suspicions that occasionally nagged at him—and Madison was exactly what she seemed—then she needed
to have someone around in case she required help. If
his suspicions turned out to be right and Madison
was a plant by the cartel, then Rosalie would undoubtedly notice something amiss in the woman's
behavior and report back to him. Rosalie was nothing
if not sharp.

He wished that he felt the same way about himself
right now.

It was after one before Duncan let himself in. All
the lights in the house, except for the one illuminating the driveway, were out. He figured it was safe to
assume that everyone was asleep. He sighed, pock-
eting his key.

The quiet felt good after the day he'd put in. It
was maddening to see how slowly the wheels were
turning on this thing, almost as slowly as the setup

for the bust itself. He was beginning to think they'd be lucky to get the case to a grand jury in less than a month. From where he stood, a month seemed like an endless stretch of time.

When he'd arrived at work this morning, and later when he'd gone out for lunch, he'd found reporters laying siege to the building. When they'd spotted him leaving, they'd swarmed, reminding him of piranha in a feeding frenzy. He hadn't gotten ten steps before reporters were aiming their microphones and their cameramen at him. It seemed he'd been elected flavor of the month. He couldn't wait until the month was over.

But it hadn't been his desire not to run into vigilant reporters that had him lagging behind at the office. And it wasn't the mountain of paperwork. Whatever he had to do could just as easily be done from home. More easily.

No, the reason he'd stayed so late was to avoid having to see and deal with Madison. Not after last night. Kissing her had been a stupid move on his part. He didn't make stupid moves very often, but that had definitely been one.

Rather than turn on the chandelier in the foyer, Duncan made his way to the stairs in the dark. He didn't want to take a chance on waking up anyone. He wasn't in the mood for conversation.

He stifled a yawn. He hadn't realized how tired he was until now. As he reached the landing, he thought he heard a faint noise. Moaning? Crying? He turned his head to listen. Was that Neil? The baby's room was next to Madison's and directly across from his own.

The door was slightly ajar and a faint pool of light

from the lamp Madison kept on had trickled into the hallway. The noise came again, more of a whimper than a cry. It was definitely coming from Neil's room.

His fingertips on the door, Duncan slowly pushed it open and looked in. The first thing he saw was the crib. He smiled to himself in satisfaction. It had arrived. Before leaving this morning, he'd left a note for Rosalie instructing her to get a crib, clothes and whatever else was necessary for Neil. There was no point in the infant sleeping in a drawer like some homeless waif and no reason why, while he was staying here, Neil couldn't enjoy some of the finer benefits of life. Life would be hard enough on the boy all too soon.

A slight breeze stirred the curtains at the window. They'd been left drawn back. Moonlight made its way into the room like a last-minute guest, mingling with the faint light coming from the small lamp and casting miniature spotlights about the room.

Neil was on his stomach, his legs tightly bunched up against him. A tiny frog in the middle of the pond. The infant was fast asleep.

Giving in to his impulse, Duncan entered the room and crossed to the crib, pulled there by an invisible magnet. He smiled as he leaned over the railing.

For a moment, Duncan lingered over the crib, watching Neil and listening to the baby's even breathing. The sound was incredibly soothing and almost as captivating as watching such a small bundle of humanity do something as mundane as sleep.

Before he could think to stop himself, Duncan reached over and gently stroked his forefinger along Neil's cheek.

The baby stirred, then sighed softly. Whether that was a coincidence or a direct response, Duncan didn't know. It didn't matter. The effect on his heart was the same. He fought the temptation to lift the sleeping baby in his arms and hold him.

The unexpected reaction surprised him. He wasn't given to sentimentality, certainly not to feeling anything remotely like this when it came to children. Maybe it was the lack of sleep.

He shook the sensation off. Then, because spring nights could turn cold without warning, Duncan took the small comforter draped over the side of the crib and placed it over the small sleeping form. He grinned to himself when he saw that the fluffy lamb cavorting across the comforter had landed so that it covered the small butt that was raised in the air.

Turning away from the crib, Duncan saw that Neil wasn't alone in the room.

On the bed, in much the same belly-to-mattress position as her son, was Madison. Also sound asleep.

It was then that Duncan realized that the noise— soft, ambiguous sounds that broke up as they drifted into the air—were coming from her and not Neil. She was dreaming about something. The life that eluded her in her waking hours? Duncan wondered if he woke her up now, would she remember anything she was dreaming about? Would it help her remember the life she'd misplaced? Probably not.

Since the noises were faint and already fading, Duncan decided not to wake her. He preferred it that way. He wasn't accustomed to consciously avoiding people or issues, but in this case he made an exception, needing to buy himself a little time. He wanted to come to terms with a few things first.

But terms or not, Duncan stood for a moment longer, watching Madison sleep. To say he couldn't help himself would have bothered him, so he didn't attempt to explore the reasons behind the uncustomary action.

One shoulder of the peach nightgown, a nightgown he assumed came from Sheila, had slid down, letting him glimpse just the slightest bit of skin. It was hardly more than what could be seen on the street at any time, day or night, in the summer. His reaction made no sense to him. Duncan felt his stomach tighten, the way it did when he went a day without stopping to eat.

Except that the ache was more pronounced.

He needed to get to bed before his imagination ran away from him and he started hallucinating. Duncan turned to leave, then turned back again. Taking the edge of the blanket lying at the foot of the bed, he gently spread it over Madison. The last thing he needed was for her to catch something.

Then, as quietly as possible, Duncan slipped out, easing the door closed behind him.

When the lock clicked into place, Madison slowly opened her eyes. Without moving, she turned them in the direction of the closed door. And then smiled.

The ringing noise was soft, but it still managed to shatter his concentration. Duncan swore under his breath as he jerked up the telephone receiver. It didn't look as if he were going to get nearly as much done at home as he'd thought.

He'd hoped that, safely sequestered in his den, the usual interruptions would be nonexistent. He wanted to finish wording this report once and for all. Capturing the drug lords had been a great deal easier for him than writing about it.

He debated turning off the phones altogether, but Stringburne had said he'd try to reach him as soon as he learned the date for the grand jury hearing. That tied Duncan's hands for him. He had to leave the phones open.

"Hello." The barked greeting wasn't meant to encourage the recipient to launch into any sort of a conversation.

The person on the other end laughed in response, the abruptness evident in Duncan's voice apparently not making the correct impression. Within a second, Duncan understood why.

"So, Duncan, how's it going?" he heard his uncle ask. "Saw you on TV the other night. Meant to call you then, but things got in the way. You know how it is. You looked handsome as ever, I might add, but tired." Just the slightest note of seriousness entered Thomas's voice. "Are you all right?"

Duncan appreciated the show of concern. Appreciated, too, that Thomas didn't push the issue. He leaned back in his chair, tucking the telephone against his shoulder and ear as he continued to hunt for elusive keys on the keyboard.

"As all right as a person can be, hounded by the news media."

"Goes with the territory," Thomas answered needlessly. The paparazzi had never bothered him, but then he hadn't borne as much as Duncan had. He hadn't been the flamboyant MacNeill the way his brother, Duncan's father, had been. "The curse of being born to famous parents. If Dad had developed a new way to prepare brussels sprouts instead of chocolate—'' he laughed at the idea ''—you might have had an entirely different childhood. Of course, that wouldn't alter the attention you're getting now.'' Inadvertently, doing what he did best, Duncan had unleashed the very media on himself that he despised. Murphy's Law, Thomas thought. ''But that isn't the reason I called.''

Duncan tried to sound mildly interested as he sought to remember where the *m* key had last been seen. ''What is?''

''I hear you're hiding a woman at your place. About time, too.''

That caught his attention. He'd expected Thomas to say something about an upcoming stockholders meeting, not comment on Madison.

''What's your source of information?'' As if he didn't know, he thought darkly. That was the trouble with sharing a housekeeper.

''Rosalie, who else? So, when do I get to meet her?'' Thomas wanted to know.

There it was, right after the *n* key. Who made up this ridiculous keyboard, anyway? ''Rosalie?'' Duncan muttered absently, striking the key. ''You already have.''

''Don't get flip with me.'' Thomas took no offense. He knew being flippant was just Duncan's way of dealing with things. ''Save it for your superiors. I'm referring to the mystery lady.''

''You've got that right,'' Duncan murmured under his breath. He shifted the bulk of his attention to the conversation. It was the only way to end it. ''It's not what you think—''

Thomas was confident that his nephew had no idea what was on his mind. ''She's breathing, isn't she?''

"Yes—"

"Then it's what I think." Rosalie had given him all the details he either wanted or needed, not to mention a vivid description of the lady in question. Sight unseen, she had his seal of approval. According to their mutual housekeeper, Madison had the face of an angel and a soul to match. That was saying quite a lot, given that it came from Rosalie, who normally had reservations about everyone. Very few people won the woman's seal of approval, and none, to his knowledge, had ever won it so quickly.

"Let an old man have his fantasies."

Duncan allowed himself to relax, easily slipping into the comfortable relationship he enjoyed with his uncle. They could go for months without picking up the phone, but once they did, it was as if no time had passed at all. "You have fantasies about me?"

"Yes."

Duncan was kidding, but his uncle sounded serious. Tired of keeping his hands poised over the keyboard, Duncan stopped trying to type altogether and took hold of the receiver again.

"About you inviting me to a wedding," Thomas added significantly.

They'd talked about marriage and weddings once or twice, in vague, general terms. When he was a kid, Duncan had wondered why Thomas had never married. He'd had fantasies of his own, fantasies that involved Thomas adopting him. Thomas won out over his own father a thousand times over. But Thomas was married to the business; he always had been.

"You've got it," Duncan said magnanimously.

"Any wedding in particular you want an invitation to, or will anybody's do?"

"Yours, smart-ass." Good-natured affection swelled in Thomas's voice.

Duncan sighed, dragging a hand through his hair. Women were the last thing on his mind these days. Except perhaps for one, but that was for an entirely different reason from the one Thomas was alluding to. "Then I'm afraid you might have a long wait ahead of you."

"Why do you think I've hung on as long as I have? So, to get back to my original question, when do I meet this mystery lady of yours?"

Duncan frowned. She was far from his, despite his prevailing sense of responsibility at the moment. "I don't think that's a very good idea."

"Of course it is." The simplest thing would be just to come over, uninvited, but Thomas was not the kind of man who presumed things, even about his own nephew. He had no intentions of barging in— unless it was a last resort. He tried another approach. "You let Rosalie meet her. Insisted on it, so I hear."

All these years, he'd thought that Rosalie was closemouthed. A lot he knew, Duncan thought.

"Then you also know why I insisted."

Thomas knew all about the baby, was eager to see the infant Duncan had helped bring into the world.

"What I know is that you're intent on tormenting an old man."

Duncan was well aware that Thomas only made use of the adjective in reference to himself when he was after something.

"Fifty-seven isn't old," Duncan reminded him.

Thomas hadn't thought that—once. But lately, he

was beginning to feel his age and then some. He was also beginning to feel antsy, as if there were a finite limit to time. "It is if you're waiting for someone to get on with their life and begin a family."

Now Thomas was beginning to sound like the kind of mother Duncan had never had. Despite himself, he grinned.

"You're all the family I need, Thomas." He paused, wondering how to phrase this next part. It wasn't easy telling someone you cared about that there might be someone looking to hurt them. But this had been on his mind ever since the threatening letter had turned up.

There was no way to say this but directly. "Thomas, I got a letter the other day. It threatened my family."

Thomas quickly filled in the spaces. "So you're worried about me. Don't be. I'm surrounded by a loyal bunch of people who've been around me for years. I'll be all right. It's you I'm worried about."

"I've had death threats before." Duncan dismissed the threat. It was no more annoying than one of the so-called fan letters he'd received.

Duncan had misunderstood him. Thomas was quick to set him on the right track. "It's your life, not your death, I'm worried about. It's time to do something other than work. Trust me, I know. This woman—"

Duncan cut his uncle off before he could continue. "This woman is a stranger who's only here because I caused the accident that gave her amnesia."

So he'd paid for her care at the hospital and had now taken her in, Thomas thought. Rosalie hadn't said anything about there being a time limit. "What are you planning to do with her?"

Keep my distance. "Help her if I can," Duncan replied matter-of-factly. "I'm still having some missing person leads followed up." He'd gone back to Kelly with a photograph he'd taken of Madison and asked him to give the search another shot. It was currently going nowhere, but he didn't feel like mentioning that to his uncle. "And the doctor who examined her ran some tests at the hospital and said her memory could come back at any time."

All true, but Thomas knew that Duncan always had a contingency plan. He wanted to hear what it was. "And if no one claims her and her memory doesn't come back, what then?"

The question had nagged at Duncan in the wee hours of the night. He couldn't see himself throwing Madison out on the street, yet she couldn't remain here indefinitely, either.

"I'll face that just as soon as the grand jury hearing is out of the way."

Duncan had too much to deal with, Thomas thought. But the boy had always done that to himself, ever since he'd been an adolescent. He seemed bent on keeping too busy to have time to think. Thomas felt it was to block out the emptiness that was, at bottom, haunting his nephew. The only trouble was, until Duncan faced the emptiness, he couldn't begin to fill it.

Thomas knew it was futile to allude to any of this. Duncan would do what he wanted to do. He always had. All Thomas could do was stand by him, no matter what. "If you need anything—"

"I'll know where to call," Duncan assured him.

It went without saying that he could always count on Thomas. It was a good feeling.

Saying goodbye, Duncan broke the connection. It never ceased to amaze him that Thomas and his father could have been related.

He'd taken the morning off because it was easier to work at home than to go into the office and face the legion of reporters who seemed bent on milking both the news of the breakup of the largest drug cartel on record and the ridiculous title he'd been awarded. The media was having a positive field day, making him out to be some sort of suave spy instead of just a man who was good at what he did.

The call from Thomas had made him restless. Sensing that he could do with a break, Duncan came out of the den he'd turned into an office and went downstairs. All he wanted was to grab a cup of coffee and maybe something to eat. He didn't particularly care what.

He found that he was still trying to adjust to a normal life after two years of living by his wits and being, in effect, a completely different person. The persona he'd invented was a great deal more open, at least to outward appearances, than he was. And a great deal more volatile. It had been, to his way of thinking at the time, a triumph of playacting. But now he wasn't so sure. Could he have been so convincing if part of him wasn't like the man he pretended to be?

For a man who had always kept his emotions and feelings tightly in control, it was a disconcerting notion to entertain. And he wouldn't have been entertaining it at all if it hadn't been for Madison and the other night.

He saw her as he walked by the living room. Her back was to him and she was sitting on the sofa. For a moment, he thought of turning around and going back upstairs, but there was something cowardly about that. Walking in, he realized that she was still unaware of his presence and with good reason.

Madison was breast-feeding Neil. Her eyes on her child, she was murmuring something that Duncan couldn't quite make out, but sounded like a lyric from a song. She looked positively radiant to him. Completely captivated by what he saw, he couldn't take his eyes from the perfect union of mother and child.

This was an intimately private moment. Duncan knew he should turn around and leave as silently as possible to spare both of them embarrassment. Instead, he remained where he was, hardly breathing, awed not so much by the scene as by the love that was so evident. He'd grown up totally unaware that such a bond could exist. In essence, his parents had remained strangers to him. Strangers with his surname.

Duncan was filled with an emotion he was hard-pressed to identify. It wasn't jealousy, it wasn't even wonder. The closest he could come to putting a name to it was yearning.

But that was ridiculous. How could he yearn for what a small child had?

Madison raised her eyes and looked at him. There was neither surprise nor reproach in her glance, but Duncan still felt like a deer caught in the sights of a hunter. Annoyed with himself for behaving like some Peeping Tom—even though that wasn't remotely close to what motivated him—he looked away.

Time and again he'd been able to talk his way out of tight situations where his very life was on the line. Inexplicably, his gift deserted him when he felt he needed it most. He'd intruded where he had no business being and had no excuse to offer for his behavior. When he tried to frame an apology, the words wouldn't come.

"I'm sorry—I didn't mean to—it was just that—" God, but he sounded stupid. If this had been Bogotá, he'd have been dead by now. He squared his shoulders, as if accepting blame she wasn't voicing. "I shouldn't have walked in on you like this. I'm sorry."

Madison slipped the receiving blanket over her shoulder, covering herself. Somehow, it didn't occur to her to be embarrassed, but seeing her like this obviously embarrassed Duncan. She adjusted the blanket to make him feel more comfortable.

"No, don't go," she called after him. Duncan turned to look at her. "This is your house. You have a right to be wherever you want. I'm the one who's sorry." With a bemused expression, he slowly crossed back to her. Madison smiled encouragingly at him. "I didn't mean to make you uncomfortable. I didn't know you were home." She would have fed Neil in his room had she known. "Rosalie said you went to work."

"Rosalie was mistaken." Not knowing what to do with them, Duncan shoved his hands into his pockets. He hadn't felt this awkward since before puberty. Perhaps not even then. He looked for an excuse to walk away. "Can I get you anything? Is there anything you need?"

The man was like her own personal fairy godmother, Madison mused. Besides the crib, he'd had baby clothes and enough diapers to cover the entire city sent over yesterday. Anything she might have thought necessary was already here.

Except for one thing. "I need you to look less uncomfortable around me."

"I'm not uncomfortable." It was a lie. Duncan paused. Things needed to be cleared up. He didn't want her thinking he'd brought her here with an ulterior motive. "About the other night. I don't want you to think that I was taking advantage of the situation."

Was that what was bothering him?

"You weren't. I was the one who said you could kiss me if you wanted to," she reminded him. "I'm not sorry that you did." She looked at Duncan, trying to read his eyes. "Are you?"

Her expression was completely guileless. Were there really people like her around, or was that just due to the amnesia? "No, but—"

"Then there's no reason to apologize." For her, it was as simple as that. "I certainly don't want you to feel uncomfortable around me. If anything, I should feel uncomfortable with you because you've been like an answer to a prayer and I don't have any way to pay you back—yet," she emphasized. "If it weren't for you, Neil and I would be in some homeless shelter right now."

"If it weren't for me, you would still have your life right now," he countered.

They both had a point, Madison thought. "We could argue this all day. Why don't we just agree not to feel awkward around each other and go from there? Deal?"

"Deal." Duncan took the hand she offered, being very careful not to dislodge the blanket draped over her breast. It was done as much to guard his sanity as to protect her modesty. A man should only have to face so much to test his resolve.

He looked as if he were going to leave again. "Why don't you stay and talk to me?" Deftly, Madison slipped her son's mouth from her breast. Cradling Neil against her shoulder, she gently patted his back, coaxing out a burp. "Neil's probably going to fall asleep again and I'd love the company, if you don't mind. I've just about talked Rosalie's ears off."

Duncan supposed, all things considered, he could spare a few minutes. Uncertain about the wisdom of this, he sat down beside her.

Ten

The quiet rap on his door caught Duncan's attention the instant he heard it. The sound was soft, as if whoever was on the other side hesitated to intrude on his solitude. He finished knotting his tie and crossed to the door.

When he opened it, he found Madison standing in the hall. She looked as if she would rather be somewhere else. Considering that in the two weeks she'd been here, she'd effortlessly woven her way into his life so that it felt as if she belonged nowhere else, Duncan found his suspicions aroused.

Habit had him glancing behind her. The hall was empty. "Anything wrong?"

What was wrong, Madison thought uncomfortably, was that she didn't really know how to broach this without coming across like someone who was bent on soaking her benefactor. "Rosalie isn't feeling well—"

Duncan shrugged into his jacket. "Is she sick?"

"She says she isn't, but she seems pretty miserable."

He wasn't sure he saw what the problem was. If it wasn't serious, why was Madison coming to him with this just as he was about to leave for work? "Does she want to see the doctor?"

"No, but I have to."

She'd made appointments with both Dr. Pollack and the pediatrician Sheila had recommended, a Dr. Rafe Saldana. She'd made them for the same day to save time and effort. But now, with Rosalie sick, she had no way of getting there. Her car had been repaired and was sitting housed in Duncan's garage, but the odd thing was, she couldn't remember how to drive.

"The two-week checkup," she explained quickly when a line of concern creased his forehead. "Rosalie was supposed to take me and I don't want her going out, feeling the way she does. I thought I might drive myself, but I can't seem to remember what to do when I'm behind the wheel." Frustrated, she took a breath, hating the way this felt. "Could I have some cab fare? I know my tab is rising, but—"

Duncan had stopped listening. He was doing a quick mental tally of his schedule. There was nothing that couldn't be postponed for a few hours at the very least. Now might be a good time to take one of those vacation days he was so top-heavy with—or at least part of one.

"What time is your appointment?"

"Appointments," she corrected. "Mine is for nine, Neil's is for ten."

"You made both for the same day?" She was efficient, even without her memory. Duncan couldn't help admiring that.

"Seemed like the logical thing to do."

That, too, he found admirable. Glancing at his watch, Duncan made up his mind. "All right, why don't you go get Neil ready."

She moved out of his way as he walked out of his room. "You'll give me cab fare?"

He thought she'd understood his meaning. "No, I'll take you myself."

Madison followed him to the landing. "You?" She hated taking him away from his work. He always seemed so busy. "Why?"

He smiled, then repeated what she'd said to him. "Seems like the logical thing to do."

"No," she contradicted, "the logical thing would be to give me cab fare."

Okay, so she had a point, but he was in no mood to concede it. "Do you have to argue with me every time I offer to help you out?"

She grinned. "No, I don't have to."

The grin was infectious, as was the woman wearing it. He felt his own lips twitching to mimic the expression. She was doing it again, he thought, taking his edge off. He couldn't just be direct and forge ahead the way he was accustomed to doing. She kept impeding his progress, buttonholing him with observations, details. With views from his backyard. Sitting there with her at night was getting to be a habit, as was Madison herself. One he warned himself not to slip into.

Strange how he couldn't seem to pay attention to his own words. He nodded, determined to stay on track. "Good, then get ready."

She felt like a soldier being ordered around by a senior officer. Why did he feel as if he had to balance out every nice thing he did with a display of impatience or temper? Was he afraid she was going to like him? If that was the case, she was going to have to tell him that he was locking the barn door long after the horse had been stolen.

"Are you always so surly when you're being helpful?" Her eyes teased him.

He caught himself beginning to linger. Beginning to give in to a feeling that would only mean trouble if it was allowed free rein. Duncan put a stop to it.

"Yes." The curt word hung in the air between them as he walked off.

Madison slanted a look at Duncan's face. Why *had* he volunteered to drive them when he could have just as easily put them in a cab and given her the fare? She knew it had nothing to do with money. If anything, he was generous to a fault and wanted nothing from her in return, not even her gratitude. He was driving her for another reason. Madison hadn't the vaguest idea why.

She didn't have many ideas when it came to the man in the driver's seat. Duncan MacNeill didn't give her much to work with. What he did give were mixed signals. One moment he was the essence of kindness, the next he disappeared from her life for several days. One second he was being gruff, the next he was making sure that she and Neil were covered while they slept.

And the kiss. The kiss that he had subsequently apologized for had been simply wonderful. It warmed her at night when she relived every stimulating second of it. Made her ache in the dark, wanting more. But he hadn't tried to kiss her again.

Why?

Didn't he want to? How *did* he feel about her? Was it strictly a matter of his feeling responsible and nothing more? If that was true, he wouldn't be beside her now, driving her to her appointment. He'd let someone else do it.

She didn't begin to understand him. Madison only knew that she was drawn to him. Very strongly. Whether gratitude or something else had colored her perception, she wasn't sure, but she did know that she felt something whenever he entered the room, something that seemed to bloom inside of her, growing larger every day.

Like a flower, she thought, being pushed out into the sun. Except in her case, the sun spent a great deal of time being overcast.

So far, the trip to the medical complex was being made in complete silence. Madison had a feeling that if she didn't speak, Duncan wouldn't, either. Silence didn't seem to bother him. It bothered her. She wanted to hear the sound of his voice.

Leaning forward slightly, Madison peered at his face. "I appreciate you bringing me here, but don't you have other things you should be doing?"

"Ducking reporters and pacing," he enumerated. "Neither of which I'm particularly patient with or good at." He noted that his answer didn't satisfy her. "I've accumulated enough personal time to take off the rest of the year if I wanted to."

She couldn't visualize Duncan kicking back and doing nothing for that duration. Madison glanced at him before looking back at the road. "You'd go crazy inside a week."

She said it as if she knew him. As if she'd made a study of him. Fragments of his dormant suspicions returned, snagging his attention. Why couldn't he make up his mind about her?

He took a right turn, sparing her a glance as he

guided the car into one of three parking lots. There were five medical buildings in the complex. Sheila's, according to the address he had, was the closest to the street.

"What makes you say that?" he asked her, his voice purposely conversational.

Madison got out to undo Neil's tethers, but Duncan was there just ahead of her. The man was fast, she mused. And his hands looked so capable, so strong, yet when he lifted Neil, he did it with the utmost gentleness. She wondered if he was aware of that, of being gentle, and whether he'd deny it if she mentioned it to him.

Probably.

"Just watching you," she answered. Duncan looked at her, waiting for more of an explanation than that. "You've got all this pent-up energy. I think if you were forced to go on a vacation, without some covert reason behind it, you'd be bored out of your mind."

Maybe she was just speculating. And maybe not. Duncan needed more information on her, more than just the gut response he was having. That was one of the reasons he'd opted to drive her to her appointments. What he needed to help him make up his mind was to spend more time with Madison instead of less. After the night following the evening he'd kissed her, he'd changed his tactics for that very reason. But the line between logical procedure and a creeping desire to spend time with her for no reason at all was beginning to blur. Telling himself that his reaction to her was purely physical and that he was a normal male, nothing more, didn't carry as much conviction with it as it should have.

Conviction notwithstanding, he needed to know if the woman who had happened into his life was there purely by accident or by orchestrated design.

He'd never been an armchair researcher. Hands-on was the only way he knew how to deal with anything. Being in the field, this time around, meant interacting with her. And Neil. Bringing them to their respective doctors seemed like a neutral enough scenario from where he stood.

Duncan hadn't counted on the way he'd feel escorting Madison. Hadn't thought about how he'd feel carrying Neil in his arms. It wasn't something he could just gloss over. Walking beside her, holding the baby in his arms smacked of a domesticity he was not acquainted with. A domesticity that, though foreign, seemed oddly right, as if it belonged in his life. It was absurd, yet he couldn't get away from the feeling, just as he couldn't get away from the feeling created within him when he'd kissed her. A feeling that had lingered on his mind far too long. Thinking about her was beginning to interfere with his clarity.

He looked down at Neil's face. The boy's eyes seemed to lock with his. Something that looked like a smile was on the small lips. Duncan found himself smiling back. He could get used to this sort of thing, he realized.

Which was exactly why he refused to. Like almost everything else in his life, this was just an illusion, something conjured up purely for effect. If he hadn't let himself get caught up in the persona the DEA had created for him—Mike St. James, big-time drug dealer—a performance that had lasted for almost two years, he wasn't about to let himself buy into this tiny slice of the American dream that had only been going on for the last two weeks.

No matter how much something within him seemed to respond to it.

He'd seen firsthand that domestic happiness didn't exist. It hadn't worked for his parents, and on the outside, they had everything on their side. Looks, family, money. But it had turned out to be a sham, a hollow shell. The illusion of happiness usually was.

So if the woman walking beside him had hair that smelled of some flower he couldn't place, if her face drifted through his mind at odd moments, it made no difference at all. It was all just part of the same illusion.

"You're probably right," he finally agreed as they stepped into the elevator. Madison pressed the button for the eighth floor. The doors closed again. They were the only passengers. "Vacations aren't for me. I like keeping busy, doing something."

"Dangerous," she added, her eyes laughing at him when he raised his brow at the word. "It has to be something dangerous that you're doing. Just doing 'something' isn't good enough."

"Dangerous," he repeated, at once a little amused and a little uneasy at the way she seemed to have his number. "Like bringing a woman in for her two-week checkup."

She winked broadly. "Depends on the woman."

Yes, Duncan thought, looking at her, it certainly does.

"You look like a fish out of water."

Madison's breath tickled his cheek as she leaned

into him to whisper the observation. His stomach muscles contracted in response.

Duncan saw no reason to argue with her assessment. There were four other women in Sheila Pollack's waiting room besides Madison. Three of them were pregnant, one of whom looked even larger than Madison had on the night he'd run into her.

Shifting in his seat, Duncan had to admit that he'd felt more comfortable in his time. Waiting for a drug dealer in a shadowy Bogotá alleyway came to mind.

"Madison?"

They both turned as the nurse called her name. Madison rose, then paused long enough to place her arm on his shoulder. For a glimmer of a moment, it felt as if their roles were reversed.

"Are you sure you'll be all right?" she asked him, glancing toward Neil. He was dozing in the baby seat she'd brought with her.

"Sure. What's he going to do? Coldcock me?" He realized she didn't know that meant being hit on the back of the head. "Never mind, I'll explain later." He indicated the nurse. "Don't keep the lady waiting."

Neil opened his eyes the moment the door closed behind Madison. Murphy's Law, Duncan thought. He supposed, if he were a betting man, he would have laid odds on that happening.

"She'll be back," he told Neil.

Neil didn't seem to believe him. When random fussing turned to cries, Duncan undid the belt restraining the infant and picked him up. Even if observation hadn't been second nature to him, Duncan would have been acutely aware that every pair of eyes in the room was on him.

Emulating what he'd seen Madison do, Duncan stroked Neil's back. The wails faded to whimpers. When he began rocking Neil against his shoulder, the whimpers disappeared altogether.

The woman sitting directly across from him caught his eye intentionally. Duncan noted the wistful look on her face. Laying her hand on her swollen belly, she leaned forward and asked in a very audible whisper, "Do you give lessons?"

He hadn't the slightest idea what she was talking about. "Excuse me?"

"Do you give lessons?" she repeated. There was a fond smile on her lips. It wasn't meant for Duncan. "My husband could stand to learn a few things from you." The woman looked down at her stomach. "This is our third baby and he still doesn't know his way around a newborn."

"It's probably just an excuse," the woman on Duncan's right volunteered. "Tell him to practice by cradling a football."

"No way." The first woman laughed. "He's liable to try to make a forward pass with the baby if I do that." She looked at Duncan again. Neil was asleep and drooling on his shirt. "Your wife's a very lucky lady."

He was about to correct her, then let it go. There was no point in saying that Madison wasn't his wife. If he did, it might open up a whole new avenue of speculation that he had no desire to get involved in. It was simpler to let her believe that he and Madison were married.

The only nonpregnant woman in the room had been staring at him intently since she'd walked in, as if she were trying to place him. She took advantage of the momentary lull in the conversation to confide, "I know this sounds dumb, but I have the strangest feeling that I know you."

"You too?" The first woman's expression lit up, animated. She seemed relieved to find someone else with the same feeling. "I'm sorry, but are you anyone famous?"

"The news." Clearly latching onto the thought, the second woman pointed excitedly at Duncan. "You were on the news last week."

The light dawned. "That's right. You're the undercover agent." The first woman looked at Neil, then back at Duncan. "Looks like you did a lot of things undercover."

"Hey, wait a minute." The woman who'd suggested using a football looked at him, confusion taking over her features. "Aren't you also *Prominence Magazine*'s World's Most Eligible Bachelor for this month?"

Oh God, not again, Duncan thought. He wondered if Madison would think to look for him out in the hall if she came out and didn't find him in the waiting room. He didn't want to hang around for what was to come.

Just then, the door leading to the examination rooms opened.

"She's all yours, Duncan."

The cavalry had arrived in the slender form of a doctor in a white lab coat instead of the young nurse who had taken Madison in. Relieved, Duncan was on his feet immediately. Neil whimpered, protesting the sudden movement. Duncan saw the amused look in Sheila's eyes. As if he'd been caught holding hot contraband, he quickly passed the baby to Madison.

Sheila made no effort to hide her amusement at his discomfort. He looked good this way, she thought. His career choice might have kept him busy, but it hadn't filled the void she knew existed within him. Maybe this was what he had needed all along.

"You've been taking very good care of her." She patted Madison's arm. "She's made a wonderful recovery. All systems are go." Sheila's eyes shifted toward Neil, cradled in his mother's arms, his small lashes fluttering shut again. Babies never ceased to tug at her heart. "They are adorable at this stage, aren't they?"

"Sometimes," one of the women in the room spoke up, her eyes on Duncan rather than Neil, "they're adorable at any stage."

Sheila knew that look. Had seen it trained on her own husband by women who were openly envious of her. She placed her hand on Duncan's shoulder as if to usher him out.

"Off you go before you cause a riot in my waiting room." The frown tickled her. She had a hunch that Gibraltar was finally coming around. "Oh, by the way, I wrote a prescription for Madison. Fill it, will you?" She tucked the small folded piece of paper into his breast pocket, then patted it as if to ensure it stayed in place. "And you still have an open invitation to our place," she told him. She smiled at Madison. "Both of you."

Turning, she called, "Betty?" The first woman who had spoken to Duncan rose awkwardly to her feet. Sheila held the door open for her. "Let's see how you're coming along."

Glancing in Duncan's direction, Sheila watched the threesome leave. Duncan and Madison made a

nice couple, she mused. Ever since she'd married
Slade, she had begun to see the entire world that way,
in terms of couples. Duncan wasn't an easy man to
be around, but he had been through a great deal,
especially when he was younger. Not every wound
had to be a physical one. He deserved to find someone to make him happy. From what she'd witnessed
so far, memory loss or not, Madison seemed to be
up to the job.

At the very least, the woman needed a last name.
Madison MacNeill had a nice ring to it, she thought.

"I'll see you soon," Sheila called after them as
she closed the inner door.

"This isn't a prescription." Duncan had waited
until he'd brought Madison and Neil to Dr. Saldana's
office, located on another floor in the same building,
before opening the paper Sheila had slipped into his
pocket. He couldn't have said exactly what prompted
him to look at it, since he hadn't a clue what sort of
medicine a new mother needed. It was probably just
habit. He was accustomed to scrutinizing every scrap
of paper that came his way—just in case.

But the words on the paper, written in a very tidy
hand that seemed light-years away from the scribble
most doctors allowed themselves, had nothing to do
with any medicine that a pharmacist would fill.

Sitting beside him, Madison leaned closer to
glance at the paper he was holding. "She wrote it on
her prescription pad. What is it?"

In response, Duncan folded the paper in half. What
Sheila had written was that he should take Madison
out for dinner that night. In the corner, she'd checked
the box that stated there was to be no substitution for

the prescription. First his uncle, now Sheila. He wished people, well-intentioned or not, would butt out of his life.

Duncan shoved the so-called prescription into his pocket without letting her see it.

"It's Sheila's idea of a joke." He wasn't going to elaborate, but the look on Madison's face pulled the words right out of his mouth. "She wants me to take you out." Annoyed that he'd told her, he blew out an exasperated breath.

She cocked her head, looking at him for guidance. "I guess I lost my sense of humor along with my memory. That doesn't sound very funny to me."

The damn thing was, he couldn't make up his mind about Madison. It went beyond his suspicions about the reasons for her being in his life. The woman herself confounded him. One moment, she seemed exceedingly competent, the next she was this lost waif he felt incredibly responsible for. And beneath all that, running like an indelible line drawn by a laundry marker, was this attraction. This steely, ever growing attraction that pulled him to her. That planted tiny vignettes in his mind, all centering around Madison.

Like tiny star bursts, they appeared at any time, without warning, to disrupt his thinking. To disrupt his own image of himself.

"Private joke," he finally muttered, looking away.

The waiting room seemed empty. There was only one other mother in the room, with a very well behaved little boy of about five or six sitting beside her. For once, Duncan would have welcomed the distracting noise. Instead of playing with the battalion of soldiers spread out on the pint-size table, the little boy was reading a book.

He reminded Duncan of himself at that age. Serious, trying very hard to fit into an adult world just to please his parents. He was ten when he gave up.

"Neil?" a young nurse called into the waiting room. She frowned as she looked at the top of the folder. "There's no last name." She looked quizzically at Duncan as he ushered Madison and Neil past her.

He saw a flicker of distress in Madison's eyes. "It's a long story," Duncan told the nurse. "The doctor knows it." He knew Saldana was a friend of Sheila's. He assumed she'd explained the matter to him.

The grateful smile Madison flashed him wasn't supposed to affect him one way or another. That it did bothered him.

Duncan wasn't completely sure, once he was inside the small, pristine examination room, what had prompted him to accompany Madison instead of remaining in the waiting room. Maybe seeing the other boy made him uncomfortable. Or maybe he just felt that as long as Neil was in his life, however peripherally, he had a right to know how the boy was doing. He didn't examine his reasons too closely. There was no future in that.

"Please undress the baby down to his diaper. The doctor will be in in a moment." Chart in hand, the nurse began to leave.

"It's kind of cold in here for that," Duncan pointed out. He saw no reason for the baby to be stripped and then left to shiver while they waited.

"Keeps the germs from multiplying," the nurse answered with a patient smile.

He hated being patronized. "Put the blanket around him when you've undressed him," he told Madison.

Madison smiled to herself. The thoughtfulness the man offered was always grudgingly given, but she was getting used to that. What mattered was that he gave it. "My thoughts exactly," she agreed.

They didn't have long to wait. Standing off to the side, Duncan observed Dr. Rafe Saldana examine Neil. He caught himself watching the man's every move as intently as he would have watched an adversary. It made no sense to him, but he couldn't shake the feeling that came over him. It was a mixture of possessiveness and a desire to protect the tiny being from any undue harm. It didn't seem to matter that Sheila had highly recommended the pediatrician, or that she entrusted the man with her own daughter's health and welfare. Duncan had always made his own judgments and relied heavily on them. It was what had kept him alive up to this point.

"Do you realize that you looked as if you were going to cut off Dr. Saldana's hand if he made a wrong move?" Madison asked Duncan after they'd returned to the car. Sitting down in the passenger seat, she slid the metal portion of the seat belt into its slot.

Duncan frowned as he started the engine. He supposed he had that coming. His first reaction, though, was to deny the observation. "You're imagining things."

"No, I'm not," she insisted easily. She knew very

little at this point, but she knew what she saw. And it had touched her. "But that's okay. I don't mind." She shifted in her seat to get a better look at his face. It looked hard as granite. But she was beginning to know better. "That is, unless you were really going to hurt the doctor. Actually, I think it was rather sweet."

He eased through a yellow light, wanting to get home. "You think hurting the doctor is sweet?"

"No, but being so protective of Neil is." He knew what she meant, she thought. He was just trying his damnedest to avoid accepting her assessment. "You're a very special man, Duncan MacNeill."

He snorted. There were a lot of people who would argue that with her. And he was among them. "Don't go fitting me for wings and a halo."

Suddenly visualizing it, Madison laughed at the image. "I don't think they would fit." Her expression softened. "But that doesn't make you any less special."

"I'm not special." He ground out the words. He didn't like her being so grateful to him. It seemed ironic, after all the pretense that he'd had to perpetrate, that he should only feel pangs over the ambivalent feelings he was having about the nature of her condition. What intensified his reaction was that he couldn't eradicate the attraction that kept slipping in, overpowering his common sense when he was least prepared for it.

He thought of the paper that was bunched up in his pocket. Filling Sheila's "prescription" would definitely play along with getting closer to Madison to see if he could find holes in her performance. To determine once and for all if she was on the level or someone he should have his guard up against.

On the other hand, by going out with her he would leave himself open to the attraction he was determined to ignore. It might become that much more entrenched in his life.

Damn it, what kind of an undercover agent was he if he wasn't up to the challenge presented by a woman who probably weighed one hundred pounds soaking wet and came up to his shoulder?

The debate was terminated. He wasn't altogether sure which side enjoyed the victory. "Would you like to go out to dinner?"

The invitation took Madison completely by surprise. And pleased her a great deal. "Decided to follow doctor's orders?"

He looked at her. There was a smile in her eyes. "Sheila has nothing to do with it."

Madison was silent for a moment, looking at him as if she were trying to make up her mind about something. "I guess not."

The car behind him honked. Duncan realized that the light had turned green. Annoyed that he hadn't noticed, he stepped on the accelerator. "What's that supposed to mean? You don't want to go out?"

"I want very much to go out with you," she answered honestly. It didn't occur to her that she should be anything else but honest with him. "No, I mean, I guess you're not the kind of man someone can order around. You don't do anything you don't want to do."

Was she trying to flatter him? "And what makes you say that?"

Madison smiled and said the age-old word that had

guided many women through the centuries. Something she had no way of knowing Duncan subscribed to himself. "Intuition."

It seemed an odd thing for a woman with no memory to say. He'd assumed that her slate was completely clean—if Madison really was what she said she was. "You have that?"

"Yes. Just like I have a sense of what goes with what in the kitchen. This amnesia thing is very whimsical." It was something that would have driven her crazy if she let it. Instead, she'd made peace with allowing things to return to her at their own pace. It seemed simpler that way, rather than trying to flush things out and be frustrated when they refused to come. "It's very selective in what I can remember and what I can't."

The narrow stretch of winding road was coming up. Duncan realized that Madison was tensing beside him. He kept her talking. "What can you remember?"

"Tiny pieces. A huge meadow. Kites."

He kept his eyes on the road. The day was clear, the sun bright. He remembered fog. "Kites?"

"Uh-huh. Big, bright red ones." Her voice grew fond as she spoke. "And a dog. One with floppy ears and low to the ground."

It sounded like a scene from a family movie—put on by a studio with a big budget, he thought cynically. "A dachshund."

"Yes." Her voice grew excited at the recognition his words sparked. "One of those."

Maybe she was remembering her childhood. "What else?"

Madison could feel the somberness encroaching. She tried to bar it. "Being afraid. Running."

He heard the change in her tone. What she was referring to worked in well with her turning up in Santa Barbara and buying the car with cash. It also fit in with her fabricating a story. Duncan still didn't know which way to play it. But a small, faint voice told him which way he wanted to. He changed the topic. "So, you do want to go out to dinner tonight?"

She smiled at him. "Yes, I do."

Without knowing why, Duncan felt like whistling. Telling himself that this all came under the heading of close surveillance didn't squelch the feeling.

Eleven

"Hey, where've you been?" Tony Fontana pushed his chair back from his desk the moment he saw Duncan enter the room. Reaching for an envelope that was on top of the clutter spread all over his desk, he held it up. "Got another for you."

Duncan knew the man wasn't talking about an ordinary fan letter. Fontana knew better than to kid him about that again. Because his home address was something that he kept strictly private, fan letters prompted by his public exposure were still turning up at the office in a more or less steady trickle. Standing orders from the captain were that the letters were to be carefully examined on the chance that another threatening letter might turn up.

Obviously, it had.

And from the looks of it, it hadn't been hard to spot. This one, like the first, had been mailed in a mint green envelope. The writer wanted to be certain his letter reached his target.

Crossing to Fontana's desk, Duncan took out a handkerchief and picked up the envelope. Using a large pair of tweezers, he drew the letter out of the envelope and scanned it. What he was looking for was a phrase, a particular wording that sounded familiar. Something that might tip him off and put a face to whoever was threatening him. He wanted to know whom he was looking for.

But there was nothing in the chillingly explicit letter that gave him the slightest clue as to the identity of the person he was up against.

Duncan raised his eyes to Fontana. "Did you read this?"

"Over and over." Fontana's expression was grave. "So did the captain." Duncan passed the letter back to him. With care, Fontana returned it to its envelope. "It's on its way to forensic, though we probably won't get anything more from it than we did the first one. Just thought you'd want to see it before I sent it off." He tapped the flap with the tweezers. "Pretty gruesome."

Duncan had already distanced himself from what he'd read. There was no other way to deal with this. "Hacking off body parts usually is."

"Doesn't it get to you, rattle you, knowing there's someone out there stalking you? Waiting for a chance to kill you and cut you up into tiny pieces?" Fontana was quoting the letter now.

Duncan started to deny it. It was purely a reflex. But then he shrugged. Maybe he was getting a little soft. "Yeah, it gets to me, but if I let it rattle me, then I'm out of the game."

Fontana snorted, slipped the envelope into a large, clear plastic bag and secured the end before going to deliver it. "Some game."

Duncan took a thick folder out of his drawer and locked it again. "You said it."

When Fontana saw Duncan begin to leave, he stopped short of the doorway. "Hey, you're not sticking around?"

''Not tonight. I've got a dinner...'' Duncan had almost slipped and said ''date.'' But it wasn't a date, it was just dinner. Nothing more, just a meal. To study a possible adversary. Stymied, he finally said, ''Engagement.''

Fontana laughed, shaking his head. ''That's what I like about you, MacNeill. You've got class. The rest of us poor working stiffs just have dinner. Maybe even a dinner date, if we're particularly lucky that night. You—you've got an 'engagement.'''

Duncan frowned at Fontana's poor imitation of an English accent. He didn't have time to hang around and listen to this. ''Call me if any more letters arrive.''

Fontana gave him a mock salute. He had a forensic expert to see. ''Will do.''

Standing in the foyer, Madison felt her mood change from hopeful to slightly daunted. Working the edge off her disappointment, she glanced down at the dress she'd put on just for him. It was one Sheila had sent over. A shimmery turquoise, the dress came up to mid-thigh and was far too pretty for everyday use.

He was a hard man to second-guess, she thought. She'd been certain that this would make him sit up and take notice. Instead, Duncan was looking at her as if he were studying a map, pondering how to get from here to there.

''You don't like it.''

Duncan looked at the sheath Madison had on. She'd turned completely in a circle for his inspection. The dress adhered in all the right places, and for the mother of a two-week-old infant, she had an incredible number of right places.

He blew out a breath slowly, hoping that would negate the slight acceleration of his pulse. He hadn't thought that the sight of a beautiful woman could take his breath away, but he was wrong.

But it wasn't simply because she looked beautiful right now. He'd been around more beautiful women wearing costlier clothing—designer labels whose price tags rivaled the military allowances for small Third World nations. But theirs had been a perfectly made-up beauty, enhanced and refined by colors gotten from jars, pots and artistically applied brushes.

That wasn't the case here. None of those women could have held a candle to the natural beauty he saw shining in Madison's eyes, the beauty he saw glowing on her face. She made him think of a spring morning, all fresh and new.

And her hair—her hair cascaded about her face and shoulders in tempestuous waves. It made him want to tangle his fingers in it, bring her face close to his until her lips were just a breath away, her heart a beat away from his.

He wanted to kiss her. He wanted, he suddenly realized with unnerving clarity, to make love with her. Wild, exotic love that washed over him like a raging sea. Soft, gentle love, like the whisper of the mist along a tile roof.

Damn, what was happening to him? Exercising the cool control that had become the hallmark of his life, Duncan slid his hands into his pockets. Only when they were hidden did he fist them. Hard.

"Yes, I do," he protested quietly, a hint of a smile

slipping over his lips without his knowledge or consent. "I like the dress very much."

He liked the woman wearing it more. Even though he knew nothing about her except what he witnessed with his own eyes, he still couldn't seem to help his reaction to her.

How was it possible that no one had noticed that this woman was missing from their life? How could she have stepped out of her life and not left a huge void behind in her wake?

Who was she? And was it just whimsical fortune that had sent her directly into his path or something else, something more? Something deadly?

He wished he could find evidence to help him make up his mind one way or another. But Frank Kelly, working on his own time at the precinct, was still drawing a blank on Madison. She didn't seem to be anyone's daughter, anyone's sister, anyone's wife or mistress. She was only someone's mother.

And Duncan's fantasy.

But that was something he wanted to keep tightly under wraps. It was bad enough that he had admitted it to himself.

Her smile reached into places within the foyer that the light from the chandelier couldn't begin to touch. She looked relieved at his answer. "Good, I wanted to please you."

"Why?" Like a man going under, he held tightly to his suspicions. Why would what he thought of her dress matter to Madison? He was no one to her.

Madison cocked her head, studying his frown. He really didn't understand, did he? Didn't know how grateful she was to him. And how drawn she was to him. Every day he pulled her in a little more with each small, uncalculated kindness he rendered.

"Because I just did. I do," she emphasized softly. "It's important." She was standing on the threshold of a brand-new, unblemished world. A world that she was free to form any way she wished. She liked the endless, unexplored possibilities that lay ahead of her. She liked what she saw in his face even more. "If I never get my memory back, this is going to be my first date. I want it to be just right."

First date. Duncan shrugged the words away, not wanting to get tangled up in their implications. "Whatever you say." He glanced at his watch. "Reservations are for seven." A thought occurred to him. Rosalie was still sick. "Who's staying with Neil?"

His concern about Neil pleased Madison far more than his appreciation of her dress.

"Angela." Rosalie had asked her youngest daughter to baby-sit Neil tonight.

"Angela?" he repeated. "Who's Angela?"

It surprised her that he didn't know. He seemed like such a stickler for knowing everything that was going on around him. "Rosalie's daughter. Her youngest," she added.

It was only because of Madison that Duncan even knew Rosalie *had* children. He had absolutely no knowledge of their names or how many of them there were. The information had never been important for him to have.

Since this Angela was Rosalie's daughter, he supposed it was all right. But he wanted to see the woman for himself before he left. "Where is she?"

"Right here." Angela, a small, dark-haired girl

with golden skin, emerged from the living room. A brighter, far younger version of her mother, Angela was holding Neil against her with the ease that came from years of experience. "Don't worry." Her words were addressed first to Duncan, then to Madison. "All my sisters ask me to baby-sit their kids. There's nothing I don't know about taking care of babies."

"I'm not worried," Madison told her. Rosalie wouldn't have asked Angela to watch Neil if the girl wasn't capable.

Duncan was not nearly as optimistic about the situation as Madison. A great deal could go wrong in a very short amount of time. He took a card out and handed it to Angela. "If anything comes up, this is the number to my cell phone. Call." It was an order.

The girl nodded, slipping the number into the front pocket of her jeans. Duncan supposed that, all things considered, she appeared competent enough. At least to place the call to him if necessary.

"Have fun," Angela told them. Already dismissing them, she cooed something to Neil, who made bubbles in reply.

Madison slipped her arm through his before he knew what she was doing. He let it remain there. It was simpler that way. And, if he was being honest with himself, more pleasant.

"I didn't realize you were that worried about Neil," she said as they went out to his car.

It went further than that. But he saw no reason to tell Madison about the threatening letters he'd been receiving. They didn't concern her. She wasn't part of his family and technically not a target. She didn't need to know that there might be someone in the shadows, stalking him. It would only worry her.

Besides, it could all be an empty threat, meant to rattle him.

Could be, but something within him doubted it. Duncan would have found it easier to shrug off the threatening letters if he hadn't dealt with these people firsthand. He knew what they were capable of. They could wipe out an entire family at first light, then eat a hearty breakfast without a single qualm.

He opened the car door for her. Across the way, on the other side of the wrought-iron fence, he saw the unmarked car. Marquez had drawn the night watch. The captain had decided it best to have someone keep a close watch on the house at all times, at least until after the grand jury had convened. Because there was Madison and the baby as well as Rosalie to consider, Duncan hadn't opposed him.

"I'm not worried about Neil," he denied. "It just always pays to be prepared." Duncan closed the door for her and rounded the hood to his side.

"Very commendable motto." And then her eyes lit up.

Like fireflies on a hot July night, he thought, then asked for the cause. "What?"

"Boy Scouts, right?" Madison could barely contain her excitement. She'd remembered something else. "That's their motto, always be prepared."

He laughed, starting the car. She looked as if she'd just won the lottery. "That's their motto," he agreed.

She talked as they drove and he found himself listening. And maybe enjoying himself just a little.

The restaurant was a posh place located on Newport Beach's stretch of Coast Highway. People came there to dine in peace and to listen to the strains of timeless music that came from a five-piece band.

Dinner was excellent. The conversation between them had been impersonal, moving forward in tiny increments. Just like, Madison surmised, a real first date might be.

Toying with the fruity drink Duncan had ordered for her when she'd asked for a taste of his scotch and soda, she leaned across the table and looked at him. "You haven't learned anything more about me, have you?"

Duncan found himself captivated by the expression in her eyes. She seemed so genuinely hopeful. The suspicions that he still harbored were growing thinner and thinner by the hour, fading like a fog along the beach as the sun grew stronger. Duncan knew firsthand that it was possible to maintain a facade over an extended period of time. He had only to look to his own life to know that. Still, he would have thought that after two weeks there would have been something to trip up Madison if this was all an elaborate ruse.

He was becoming inclined to think that it wasn't. Or maybe he just didn't want it to be.

He took a slow sip from the stocky glass, knowing he had to make this one drink last. He wouldn't allow himself two. A clear head was vital at all times. There was no such thing as downtime for him. "I would have told you if I had."

"Right." The apologetic smile she flashed was far from embarrassed. Only bewitching. "Sorry, I didn't mean to doubt you."

Sitting back, he studied her. The blush that crept up her cheeks was appealing. And arousing. He was going to have to watch himself. She was already affecting him far too much.

He pushed on, searching for facts, not reactions. "What are you going to do if your memory doesn't return?" Had she thought about that? he wondered. Had she worried over it?

She gazed down into the drink, as if there might be an answer to his question somewhere in the melting pink foam. Madison took out the tiny umbrella and licked the end of the stick slowly. The look in his eyes as he watched her made her tingle. It wasn't easy focusing on the conversation.

"Well, certainly stop living with you. Not that I don't enjoy it—what woman wouldn't—but I'm going to have to take those first steps to making a life for myself and Neil." She smoothed out the umbrella, then placed it on the napkin. "Right now, I feel as if I'm circling the airport, locked in a holding pattern."

"And you want to take off." To where? he wondered. Would a response come to her automatically? Would it carry some clue to her identity?

She thought his words over before answering. "I want to land first so that I can take off again."

She seemed so untroubled now, so willing to accept everything at face value and make the best of it. On the surface, she could lay claim to nothing, and yet she seemed happy. How was that possible? he wondered. How was it possible that she, with nothing, was happier than so many people he'd known who had everything?

"Would it bother you—" he watched her eyes closely "—never knowing who you are?"

"Was," she corrected. "Who I was. Because right

now, I'm me, with all the feelings and responses of a normal woman. And yes, it would bother me a little, not knowing," she admitted, then smiled. "But maybe it's even better this way." In her enthusiasm, she reached over and placed her hand on his. "I've got a clean slate in front of me. Maybe the life I left wasn't a very good one. Maybe that's why I can't remember. Maybe deep down, I don't want to."

She thought of the recurring dream she had. The one where she was running, crying. Every time she woke from it, there was a huge ache in her chest. That couldn't be a good sign. At the very least, it indicated to her that there was something in her past she wanted to forget.

Madison looked down at her left hand. At the empty place where a wedding ring should have been. It was more than an empty place, it was an empty feeling.

"I don't think there was anyone in my life when you found me." She raised her eyes to his. "If I had a husband, or someone who cared, they would have filed a missing person's report on me by now. And somehow, I think I would know, would feel it, in here—" she touched her breast where her heart was "—if there was someone in my life."

He couldn't argue with that. But he couldn't really understand it, either. He knew that for once he was allowing his feelings to color his perception, but he couldn't seem to keep them under lock and key where she was concerned.

"I can't see how there isn't anyone."

Madison grinned. "That's probably the sweetest thing you've ever said to me."

"I wasn't trying to be sweet—"

"Don't ruin it," she warned, a smile playing on her lips. The way he looked at her made her feel warm. The ghostly shadows of loneliness vanished. She didn't feel alone anymore. "Anyway, the evidence speaks for itself. Maybe Neil's father and I had a falling-out." She shrugged. It didn't really matter anymore. She had to deal with what she knew and not make herself crazy with what she didn't know and might not ever know. "Maybe it even happened before I knew I was pregnant." Her speculation broadened. "My parents are probably dead, or maybe estranged from me for some reason. There could be lots of reasons why I'm alone."

Duncan nodded, conceding the point. What she said was valid. But he wasn't prepared for what she said next.

"Why are you alone?"

Caught off guard, he took a minute to collect his thoughts. "My parents are both dead, but I'm not alone. My uncle Thomas is alive. He was more of a father to me than my own was, anyway."

She wanted to hear more. Needed to hear more. Moving the drink aside, she leaned her head on her upturned hand, ready to absorb every word, every nuance he had to offer. "Really? Tell me about this uncle Thomas. And you."

So many interviews had begun this way. Suspicion was too inbred in Duncan not to rise up now. "Why?"

She both hated and didn't understand the suspicion that she could see enter his eyes. Why didn't he trust her? She had given him no reason not to.

"Because I need to fill up these empty spaces that are rattling around in my head." She was hungry for life. Someone else's if not her own right now. "I know all about Rosalie and her family, now it's your turn."

He had a natural aversion to talking about himself. Shyness had little to do with it. Duncan liked keeping his own counsel whenever possible. "There's not much to tell."

Even if she hadn't seen that snippet on the news about him, Madison would have known that wasn't true. "Rosalie said you're rather closemouthed because when you were growing up, there were always reporters around, hounding you and your parents."

He refused to let any of the memories through. They belonged in the past, dead, along with his parents. As for Rosalie, he was acutely disappointed that the woman had seen fit to tell a stranger about the family.

"Oh, she did, did she?" He drained his glass. "What else did Rosalie tell you?"

Madison watched his eyes as she repeated what the housekeeper had told her. It was speculation on the woman's part, but she sensed it was all true. "That she thinks you like to take chances with your life because you felt there was never anyone there to love you. You think that you're expendable."

Duncan stiffened, though his face remained impassive. That hit far too close to home for his liking. "Rosalie has entirely too much time on her hands."

Madison wouldn't back away. If she couldn't find the truth for herself, maybe she could help him face it. "Is she right? Is that why you do it? Because there's no one who counts in your life?"

His eyes darkened. She could see that he was distancing himself from her. But when he spoke, she

realized that however true what Rosalie had told her
was, it was also part of him.

"I do it because no matter how advanced we get
technologically, there are some things that don't get
done by sitting behind a desk, pushing computer
keys. I do it so that some kid in Bakersfield won't
die from an overdose of drugs tomorrow because I
did my job and stopped the supply at the source."
He realized that he sounded as if he'd just mounted
a soapbox. It wasn't supposed to have come out that
way. "Any other questions?"

She'd come this far, she pushed a little further.
"Yes. Do you like being alone?"

"I'm not alone. I already told you, I have an uncle
I care about quite a bit."

He was being evasive and they both knew it.
"That's not what I meant."

His expression gave nothing away. "What do you
mean?"

She was tempted to study the tips of her nails, but
that would be cowardly. Instead, she met his gaze
head-on. "Well, you're very good-looking and I was
just wondering why there was no woman in your
life."

The question should have made him angry. Would
have made him angry, coming from a reporter. Instead, he laughed. "Rather direct, aren't you?"

"I haven't learned how to be subtle yet," she confessed freely.

Curiosity, once mild, rose. "What did Rosalie say
the reason was?" The women had probably dis-
cussed this, too.

"She didn't know." Madison moved her hands
out of the way when the waiter approached and in-

dicated her empty plate. The man whisked it away. "She just thought it was a shame."

Duncan nodded dismissively to the waiter, wanting him to leave. The younger man took his plate and disappeared. "What was?"

"That you don't let anyone in."

"I let you in."

They were playing with semantics now. She couldn't help wondering what it would take to earn Duncan's confidence. "Did you?"

"You're living at the house, aren't you?"

Living with and being let in were two different things. She had a feeling that any further discussion would only lead to a dead end right now. Duncan apparently cherished his privacy as much as he cherished his life. For now, she withdrew from the barred citadel.

The band was playing a song that sounded vaguely familiar. She didn't even try to place it. "Do you like to dance?"

"Not generally." As a child, he'd been subjected to social dancing lessons. He recalled agonizing hours spent dancing with a girl twice his height. At the time, he thought he'd never live through it. Or grow taller. "My parents insisted I take lessons."

Eventually, those lessons had come in handy in ways his parents had never dreamed. He'd used them when he'd gone undercover. It was amazing what a woman would confess to a man while dancing with him. Dancing was a tool, a means to a necessary end. Dancing for its own sake had never particularly appealed to him.

"Why?" He looked at her. "Do you like to dance?"

"I think so." Madison moved back her chair. "I'm not sure." As he watched, surprised, she rose. "Would you like to help me find out?"

Standing beside him now, Madison left him no choice. He sighed, then rose. Taking her hand, Duncan walked out to the dance floor, a space he judged far too small to be accommodating.

The dance was a slow one. When he took her into his arms, she nestled against him as if she belonged nowhere else. The scent that lingered in her hair drifted toward him as slowly as the music. And did more harm.

They moved as one.

Small, insistent sensations began to travel through him, heating his body, teasing him with the feel of hers. He should have refused, he thought. He didn't want to.

Madison looked up at him. "Yes."

Confusion met the single word. He didn't understand. "Yes, what?"

"Yes, I like to dance. Very much." Without another word, she rested her cheek against his chest again.

Maybe he did, too, he thought, holding her closer to him. At least, he amended silently, just this once.

Twelve

It worried him.

What he saw happening to himself worried Duncan a great deal. It was as if someone had reached inside of him and tampered with his fine-tuning. Suddenly, he couldn't focus his attention on what he was doing. The steely concentration that was as much a part of him as the color of his eyes or his strong chin was dissolving, trickling through his fingers like an ice cube that could no longer maintain its shape.

All because of a pair of wide green eyes and a slightly off-center smile that shot straight to the bone, taking no prisoners.

No, that wasn't strictly accurate, he thought grudgingly as he let himself into his bedroom. Madison had taken prisoners. She'd taken him.

Like air, she was suddenly everywhere, invading all the spaces of his mind, her presence slipping in behind each thought, bordering along the edges of everything he did.

She wasn't exactly an obsession, but she was everything up to that point. Fragments of her conversation, her laughter, low and sexy, her look, her touch on his arm, all this and more would pop up in his mind with no warning. They would suddenly just *be* there, crowding out whatever was supposed to be on his mind until it moved into the background or faded away altogether.

Annoyed, far more with himself than with her, Duncan unknotted his tie and slid it off, then tossed it aside. It did no good to pretend that this was a temporary reaction, that he was just getting caught up in the riddle that surrounded Madison. It did no good to cling to the excuse that he had a tendency to work on the pieces of a puzzle, turning them around and around until they finally fit together and say that *that* was why she was on his mind so much.

Because it would be a lie, and he knew it. There was a great deal more involved than simply wanting to find answers.

He wanted her. Wanted her in the worst way.

In the best way.

Duncan scrubbed his face with his hands, trying to get a grip. Fuzzy, disoriented, he felt like a man drugged on cold medication.

And yet...

Yet he had never felt better in his life. Never felt more alive, more alert, not even at the peak of the most dangerous situations in his life. Adrenaline would pump through his veins then, but it was fleeting. In this case, adrenaline had moved in and set up housekeeping. All he had to do was think of Madison and it was there, agitating him. Making him crazy.

Just as she was.

It had taken all the control he had within him not to follow through on those suddenly demanding, suddenly in-your-face feelings that had appeared while he was dancing with her tonight. Oh, he'd wanted women before. Had women before. But there had never been this constant, all-pervasive kind of desire involved. All the other times, there had been no feelings at all, only physical reactions. The women were there and he was there. Pleasure was had and then forgotten. It was as primal, as simple as that.

This was not simple.

He threw his jacket on the bed. When it slid formlessly to the floor, he ignored it. How could he feel this way about a woman he knew nothing about? A woman who knew nothing about herself? It didn't make any sense.

It didn't have to. It just was.

He began to unbutton his shirt. If he concentrated, he could still feel her against him, the top of her hair barely brushing along the bottom of his chin. The scent of the soap she used still clung to his clothing where she had rested her cheek while they danced. And danced and danced, until the evening somehow managed to melt away and it was time to go home.

Home. Not his *house*, but his *home*, he realized with a start, stripping off his shirt. For the first time in more years than he could remember, he actually thought of this stone castle as home. Because she was here, she was part of it.

When had it happened? How?

Duncan kicked off his shoes, then balanced first on one foot, then the other, peeling off his socks. Balling them up, he tossed them in a corner. Damn it, what was wrong with him? He knew better than to lead with his feelings.

Didn't he? Hell, until this evening, he hadn't really thought he *had* any feelings anymore.

His reflection in the mirror above the bureau caught his eye. Here he was, mentally admonishing himself, and he was smiling. Grinning like some village idiot without any reason. No, there was a reason. And the reason was down the hall, probably sound asleep by now.

Duncan dragged a hand through his hair, fighting restlessness. She'd get more sleep than he would tonight, he thought. He was wide-awake, the kind of wide-awake that came when exhaustion got a second wind. He'd tried to tire himself out after they'd returned from the restaurant by locking himself up in the den and going over some of the facts he was presenting to the grand jury tomorrow afternoon. All the effort had done was given him a headache. His mind kept returning to her. To what she was doing right at that moment. He tortured himself by envisioning Madison getting ready for bed.

Look at yourself, Duncan thought in disgust. He'd turned into a mental Peeping Tom. This had to be an all-time low for him.

Giving up, he decided that he might as well get to bed. Not that lying down would help. Not when his body felt as wound up as a coil with nowhere to spring, nowhere to release the energy that had collected. Duncan laughed disparagingly under his breath. Served him right for being gallant.

As if he'd had any other choice. Madison had looked up at him with those liquid green eyes of hers as he left her at her bedroom door and he'd known. Known right then and there that if he'd pushed open her door using even the slightest pressure from his fingertips, he would have been there for the night.

With her.

Making love with her.

Because she wanted him to. He doubted that she wanted to make love with him as much as he wanted to make love with her, because the depth and breadth of his desire were growing at a prodigious rate, but she had wanted it. He'd seen it in her eyes. Which was why he'd used every fiber of restraint at his disposal to walk away. He knew it was the right thing to do.

Right had never felt so wrong.

He needed a shower, Duncan decided. A hot one to get rid of the aches he felt in his muscles and to calm him down. But he'd take a cold one, because it was the only way to temporarily put the other aches he was experiencing on hold. He hoped.

Duncan had just reached into the shower stall to turn on the water when he heard it. A wail that bordered on a cry of fear. Abandoning the shower, he moved back into his room, listening.

Another cry came on the heels of the first, louder this time. He hadn't imagined it. Neil? No, he didn't think so. He'd just checked on the baby before he'd gone into his bedroom. Neil had been fast asleep.

Duncan stepped out into the hall as a third cry echoed along the walls. The sound wasn't coming from Neil's room. It was coming from Madison's.

He knocked on her door, but there was no answer. The only response he heard was yet another cry, softer this time, like a small animal whimpering. A small animal in pain.

"Madison?" Alarmed now, he tried the doorknob and it gave under his hand. She screamed as he opened the door.

His heart pounding, he scanned the dark room, feeling for the light switch and damning himself for not taking his gun with him.

Light flooded the room half a heartbeat later and

he realized she was in bed. Asleep. Trembling, terrified, Madison was in the grips of a nightmare.

Relieved it was no more than a dream, Duncan hurried over to her bed. He put his arms around her, physically trying to shield her from whatever it was in her dream that was frightening her. Startled, Madison clawed at his arms, her eyes still shut tight. He held on, hating whatever had put this kind of terror into her.

She was remembering, he thought. Would she remember this and more when she woke up? Would she finally know who she was when she opened her eyes?

"Shhh, it's all right, Madison. It's all right." Sitting on the edge of the bed, Duncan cradled her against him, stroking her hair. His voice was low, reassuring. "It's a dream, just a dream." She was still trembling against him. He was helpless to make her stop. There was nothing Duncan hated more than feeling helpless. "You're safe now. I've got you and you're safe."

His voice burrowed into the nightmare, breaking it apart. In her dream, she reached for him, reached for his help. Her fingers found only mist.

Madison woke up gulping air like a drowning victim being pulled out of the surf. Shaking uncontrollably, frightened by the shapeless things that had been after her, shooting at her, she clung to his bare arm with both of hers. Hanging on for dear life. Desperately, she sought for order. Slowly, her orientation took hold.

He could feel her breasts heaving beneath his arm as she tried to steady her breathing. Desire ripped through him like the aftershocks of an earthquake.

He held on to his unsteady resolve. She was already frightened; he wasn't about to make it any worse.

When she finally stopped trembling, Duncan raised her head with the crook of his finger. Her eyes, when they met his, were wet. She'd been crying. Something twisted in his chest.

"Better?" She merely nodded in reply. "What were you dreaming about?" He struggled to keep his voice even. He didn't want her to think he was grilling her, but he had to know.

Madison dragged more air into her lungs before answering. "Something was coming after me. No," she corrected. "Not something. Someone..." Madison concentrated, but nothing more came. She couldn't make out features. The only thing she could remember was the terror that had filled her. "He was going to kill me."

It was the same dream she'd had before. It was a little clearer this time, but it was the same one. She didn't want to talk about it. Taking a deep breath, she blew it out again, slowly, curving her cheek against Duncan's bare arm. Just having him here made her feel safer. "I'm sorry, did I wake you?"

He resisted the desire to stroke her hair again, then gave in. What harm would it do? "I'm not sure, but I think you woke up everyone in a five-mile radius except for Neil. That boy sleeps like a stone."

Before he realized what he was doing, Duncan bent and kissed the top of her head. Warning signals went off throughout his body, telling him to back off. Raising his head, he squared his shoulders. He had to get out of here. "You want me to get you anything? Something to drink?"

She shook her head in answer to both. When he

began to rise from the bed, she held on to his arm. She couldn't bear being alone.

"Don't go yet," she whispered.

This wasn't a good idea, he thought, sitting down again. He had to leave...before he couldn't. Duncan thought of the housekeeper downstairs, asleep in the guest room at the rear of the house.

"Maybe I'd better get Rosalie—" He stopped. He couldn't get Rosalie. Rosalie was sick.

"No, not Rosalie. You." Her eyes pleaded with him eloquently. "Please."

Duncan felt trapped. By the look in her eyes. By the desire in his own heart.

"All right." Steeling himself, Duncan tried to get comfortable on the bed. He moved back until his shoulders were against the headboard. "I'll stay for a little while."

Holding her, he felt the warmth of her body transfer to his, felt her breath skim along his skin as she rested her head against his chest. He could feel his own body tighten inch by inch.

The spring was wound past its limit. Demands were slamming against one another, clamoring for release. He wondered what gods he'd displeased to be put to this kind of test. A test he was beginning to feel he was destined to fail.

When she turned her face up to his, he knew he was on the losing side in a battle. Very gently, he tried to ease her from him. It was difficult because he didn't want to. "Madison, I think I'd better leave."

Madison bit her lip. She knew she was crossing a line, but she didn't care, because she knew what was in her heart. Tonight, when he had walked away from her when he could just as easily have had her, she knew for certain that he was a decent, good man. And she knew beyond a doubt that she was in love with him. "I don't want you to leave."

Didn't she understand what she was doing to him? That he was barely able to keep his hands off her? She was pushing him past a limit. "Madison, you don't know what you're asking for."

Her eyes held his. "Yes, I do."

He ran his thumb along her lower lip. The slight bit of moisture he felt heated his loins. He was amazed at the amount of self-torture he could endure.

"Madison, if I stay…" He tried again. Maybe telling her would make her back away, because he was beginning to doubt that he could anymore on his own. Common sense was fading fast. "Madison, I want to make love with you."

She could feel her heart beginning to pound. "I know."

She knew? Then why was she putting him through this? Why wasn't she letting him leave the room? "You've just had—"

She knew what he was about to say. That she'd just had a baby and couldn't make love with a man yet. But she was strong and the doctor had assured her that she was physically able to do anything she wanted to, including having relations. Madison had a strong feeling that Dr. Pollack knew exactly what was in her heart.

And who.

Her hands resting on Duncan's shoulders, Madison got up on her knees and faced him. Her mouth inches from his, she ended the sentence for him, but not the way he'd intended.

"A very satisfactory bill of health. Dr. Pollack—Sheila," she amended, "says I can do whatever I want." Her eyes touched his face. "And what I want to do is make love with you."

The breath in his lungs backed up so quickly he felt a tightness in his chest. He couldn't take his eyes from hers. "You're sure?"

Her smile was shy, sweet and so enticing that it hurt. "I'd say I was never more sure of anything in my life, but that wouldn't go very far, would it?"

He pulled her down onto the bed and to him. His arms bracketed her body. "Far enough."

Unable to hold himself in check any longer, Duncan kissed her. Kissed her with a longing that had been years in the making, not just weeks. Kissed her as if she were the answer to a prayer. Because she was, even though he hadn't known, until this moment, that he had prayed.

Madison could feel her body quickening as the kiss deepened, taking her spiraling to a place that was all softness and light, all fire and velvet.

Every fiber in her being wanted this, needed it. If she'd felt empty and less than whole before, that was gone now. Here, in his arms, lost in his embrace, in the exciting texture of his mouth, she felt complete. And so incredibly happy she was certain she was glowing like a flare.

His palms skimming her body, Duncan touched her as if she were something precious, something that could easily shatter at the slightest wrong move. But she didn't want reverence, she wanted to feel his hands on her, all over her.

"It's all right," she whispered against his mouth. "I won't break."

Madison caught her breath as she pressed his hand over her breast, arching into him. He cupped her, then brought his mouth down, kissing her trembling flesh. A thousand sensations danced over her, setting her on fire. He had no idea, she thought, how over-whelmingly sweet that was. And no idea what he did to her.

She moved her body into his touch, arching, ach-ing to savor it. Aching to give him the only gift she had. Herself. Anticipation joined hands with desire and raced up and down her veins, crackling like static electricity on a dry day.

It was only with the utmost care that Duncan re-frained from tearing Madison's nightgown from her body. He wanted to be gentle with her, yet there were these passions rampaging through him like pillaging Vikings through a village. He didn't want to frighten her, but, oh, what she was doing to him. He hardly knew himself. Making love with a woman had never sucked him into a vortex before, never made him feel as if he'd just walked into an oven and planted him-self squarely on a rack. Every inch of him burned. Burned for her.

She had the face of an angel and a body made for loving. The thought throbbed over and over again in his head, the rhythm it created matched by the throb-bing in his body. This was happening too fast. Too fast. And he had no idea how to put on the brakes. No desire to put them on.

If some fragment of his mind still wondered what had possessed him, why his mind was suddenly drained of all common sense, all logical thought, only to have the space filled with emotions he had no idea how to handle, he didn't dwell on it. He couldn't. His way of handling emotions had always been to lock them away, deny their existence. But he couldn't deny what was racking his soul so urgently.

With hands that felt clumsy, he lifted the nightgown from her hips, inching it up her body and replacing the fabric with his palms. Easing the cloth up over her head, he tossed the garment aside. He couldn't tear his eyes away from her. Sleek, supple, Madison lay before him, dressed only in his desire.

"God, but you are beautiful," he murmured.

As if to reassure himself that she was there, he molded her to him, glorying in the softness of her. In the feel, the scent and the excitement of her.

She might as well have been his first, he realized, for he had never felt this way before. Like a besotted, drunken young man bent on imbibing until he passed out from the ecstasy of it.

His hands were everywhere, exploring, claiming, settling. She was his and nothing else mattered. Not drug cartels or grand juries or even lies. Nothing mattered but this woman in his arms. This woman who set him on fire. His lips followed the path his hands had forged, sampling, cataloging and savoring the spectrum of tastes that were hers alone. His heart slammed against his chest when he heard her moan.

Determined to match him, to rouse his desire the way he roused hers, Madison tugged urgently at his belt. The metal tongue slipped from its confinement and she loosened it, then worked the button at the top of his trousers. She pushed it through the hole, fighting desperately to keep her mind on what she was doing as she felt herself being reduced to the consistency of rainwater. His tongue, teeth and lips were responsible for her present liquid state. They were skimming along her body, making her vibrate. Making her disappear into a world Duncan was creating for just the two of them.

Her hands on either side of his trousers, her fingers tangling in the waistband of his briefs, she pushed both off his hips. Madison sucked in her breath as she felt him against her, hard, wanting.

Duncan kicked off the confining clothes, his eyes never leaving her face. He groaned as she raised her head and pressed urgent kisses against his throat.

She felt the pulse in his throat vibrate against her lips. Delight flowed through her, sending her excitement reeling up another notch. With deft movements, their positions switched, and now she was the one over him. Her hair rained down on either side of Duncan as she raced kisses along his face, his lips, his chin. She moved her body erotically along his as she traced her lips over his chest.

Duncan tangled his fingers in her hair and brought her mouth back up to his. Her expression was of aroused innocence. How was that possible? The woman was a revelation.

Thinking himself a fair judge of character, Duncan would have never guessed that beneath Madison's sweet demeanor existed the soul of a wanton woman. There were no bounds to his excitement.

Switching positions again, he pressed her shoulders against the bed, pinning each with a kiss. He needed to feel her body, willing, fluid, moving beneath his. He needed her, and that, more than anything, would have scared him—had he been able to think.

But he wasn't.

All he was able to do was feel. For the first time

in his life, Duncan couldn't rely on his thoughts or his quick mind. All that was left of him was instincts and reflexes.

And a desire to be filled with Madison.

He couldn't get enough, not of the taste of her, the feel of her, the scent. The more he had, the more he wanted. Like a man who had lived on beggar's rations all his life, he feasted at the banquet he suddenly found himself attending.

Madison couldn't catch her breath, couldn't return what she was receiving. He was too fast, too good, too clever. And his hands, his long, delicate hands, were creating magic all along her body. He stroked, caressed, teased and, with every pass, created peaks from which she plummeted, sensations from which she could barely recover before another came in its wake.

And then, when her body, racked with pleasure, slick with feverish sweat, was poised beneath his, she looked up at him with smoky eyes that were filled with an emotion he was afraid to see.

"Did they teach you this in undercover school?" The words were coming in short, staccato bursts.

"No," he answered, a sweet ache wrenching every inch of him. He framed her face. "You did." Because it was true. Only she had brought this out of him. No one else ever had.

His eyes on hers, he sheathed himself within her, and for one timeless moment, as they ascended the crest together, Duncan thought he glimpsed his soul.

Thirteen

Duncan woke with a start. He didn't remember dozing off. With effort, he tried to peel away the effects of sleep from his brain. A soft voice whispered, "What is it?" against his ear. Voice and accompanying breath sent a warm shiver through him.

Madison.

So, it hadn't been a dream. It had been true. All of it. He'd made love with her. Taken her ripe, supple body and found his salvation, however temporarily, within the passionate sweetness she'd offered him.

It took him a moment to digest that.

"Nothing," he answered.

Shifting, he realized that his arm was still around her. It felt stiff, but that didn't matter. Duncan gathered her to him, wanting to hold on to what he'd found for a little while longer. Happiness was such a foreign state for him, he wasn't sure whether to savor it or be leery of the complacency it bred.

It wouldn't do to feel too comfortable in this state. He knew damn well that at very best it was transitory. What was left in its wake could be worse than what was there before. Still, none of that seemed quite real. Only holding Madison did.

"I must have dozed off," he admitted. The fond

smile on her face told him that she already knew that. "Why aren't you asleep?"

Madison placed her hand on his chest. His skin had a golden hue and was warm and smooth to the touch. She slid her fingers lightly down and thrilled at the increased rhythm of his heart. She did that to him. Just as he, Madison thought, did that to her.

"I'm too happy to sleep." She curled into him, then frowned thoughtfully when she saw the faint zigzag line on his right shoulder. She'd been a little too distracted to notice it before. It looked as if it had healed only recently. Catching her lower lip between her teeth, she traced the pattern with the tip of her finger. "Where did you get this?"

Duncan glanced at his shoulder, though he knew what she was referring to. The way she touched it, he could have sworn she was trying to make it better. It was a silly thought. He caught her hand in his and brought it to his lips. Away from the scar.

"That's a souvenir from Colombia. You don't want to hear about it."

He was dismissing it, and maybe her, as well. She didn't want to be dismissed. She wanted to be in every part of his life, just as she felt he was in hers. She would have told him anything—if there was something to tell.

"Yes, I do." She raised her head so that he could see her eyes. So that he could see she was serious. "I want to hear about everything that has to do with you, no matter how small."

Instead of answering, Duncan merely laughed, remembering what she'd told him earlier. "To fill up your empty spaces, right?" Tangling his fingers in her hair, he brushed it away from her face. *So nat-*

ural, so pretty. Why'd you come into my life, Madison? I was doing just fine until you came. Now everything's fuzzy.

She turned her cheek into his palm, loving the feel of his hand. Loving him. "In part."

"And in part...?" He let his voice trail off, waiting for her to fill in the gap.

"A woman should know as much as she can about the man she's in love with." She said it before her courage failed. Said it because it was true and maybe saying it would make a difference. For both of them.

Duncan looked stunned for a second, and then his eyes darkened and his expression turned stony. Though he didn't move, she could sense him withdrawing from her. It hurt a little, but it wasn't anything she hadn't expected. "Wrong thing to say, huh?" she guessed.

He opened his mouth to say something—what, he wasn't sure—but she wouldn't let him.

"Well, I don't have any feminine wiles to fall back on." Her smile was rueful. "I seem to be very depleted in that area. My feminine wiles haven't returned yet, and even if they do, I have a feeling that I don't believe in holding things back."

Apparently not. Her declaration made him uncomfortable. It placed a responsibility on him, a responsibility he didn't want or know how to handle. "Madison, you shouldn't—"

"Have said that?" she concluded for him. "Too late. Or do you mean I shouldn't love you? Also too late." She wasn't sorry she'd said it, she wasn't about to take it back even if she could. She was just sorry he couldn't enjoy it, but then, he was far more complex than she was. He got in his own way.

Duncan wanted her to take back the words. It made what had just happened between them too important. "Madison, you don't know what you're saying."

"Oh, but I do, and don't worry, there're no strings attached." Her heart went out to him. If she didn't know any better, she would have said he looked as if he were afraid. She didn't want him to be, not of her, not of love. "I don't even expect you to say it, too." A serious note drifted into her voice. She wanted him to understand that what she felt was real and he couldn't stop her from feeling it, no matter what he said. "I'm very grateful to you for everything you've done for Neil and me, for taking us in the way you have. But you can't tell me who I can and can't love, Duncan."

He seized the excuse she'd inadvertently given him. "That's just it—you don't love me. You're just grateful to me, nothing else."

Was he really that afraid of being loved? she wondered. Did he think her love would confine him somehow? Then it wouldn't be love, it would be a trap.

Madison shook her head, smiling as she rose and sat back on her heels. "Oh, but there is. There's a whole bunch more 'else' that I haven't even tapped into."

He was having trouble concentrating on what she was saying. She was sitting in front of him, completely uninhibited and completely delectable. Innocence and sexuality met and combined in her face. Duncan marveled at the marriage.

Marveled, too, that the sated feeling he'd had only

moments ago had entirely vanished. He was hungry all over again.

Ravenous.

For her.

Leaning over him, the ends of her hair brushing against his chest, Madison framed Duncan's face in her hands. Her heart felt as if it were brimming over.

"Don't be afraid to let someone love you, Duncan. You really are very lovable, you know—when you don't frown," she teased.

Oh God, if this woman only knew what she was doing to him. And what she was asking of him. Something that was beyond his power to give. "I'll break your heart, Madison," he warned. He wouldn't be able to help it. He couldn't give her what he instinctively knew she needed. Couldn't give her the kind of love she deserved. He didn't know how.

That he warned her only made Madison love him that much more. "I'll risk it. Who knows, you might turn out to be wrong. And even if you're right, I'll have a new memory to look back on."

The smile in her eyes reached out to Duncan, ensnaring him as tightly as if he'd fallen into a net and had it close off his only avenue of escape. Unable to help himself, he dragged her down to him. Every inch of him wanted her. Wanted her as badly as he had before. Maybe even more. Because before it had been just speculation; now he knew what was waiting for him. Knew and hadn't the strength to walk away.

He knew he should be drawn and quartered for what he was doing. It wasn't fair to Madison. But fair and right and wrong were only words that drifted in and out of his mind, a mind that was already beginning to shut down again. Every fiber of his soul was trained on her. On having her, making love with her. And perhaps, for a little while, filling this huge, overwhelming ache he felt. An ache he hadn't even been aware of until she'd come into his life.

Duncan ran his hands along her body, his fingers memorizing the gentle curves. Her flesh was warm and pliant, receptive and giving, just as her mouth was. There was no hint of timidity now. It amazed him that she met each move with one of her own, rained openmouthed kisses all along his body as he had done with her.

The terrain and excitement were familiar, yet the unknown still shimmered before him. Tempting him, urging him on just a little further. She was a revelation and he was there to learn.

Madison had thought that she'd experienced everything there was to lovemaking earlier, but she discovered she'd been wrong. Naively wrong. With deft applications of his lips he uncovered sweet spots she couldn't have begun to guess existed and made her body sing. She was the instrument and he the player. Any tune he desired, she'd render.

She moaned, digging her fingers into Duncan's shoulders as the first crest peaked and racked her body with sweet ecstasy. When he began again, his fingers rousing her from depths to heights in swift movements measured in heartbeats that kept time with a hummingbird's wings, she withered and twisted, her body seeking his.

"Together," she entreated in a hoarse whisper, afraid that at any moment she was going to scream and wake the baby. "Please."

He couldn't refuse her and he couldn't hold back any longer. Watching her arch and buck had made the sweat break out all over his body, had primed him and made him yearn.

With his body hovering over hers, he entered her and bit off a groan as he felt her tighten around him. The rhythm came without thought, without being summoned. It was a part of him, just as she would always be, no matter what paths life took them on. He didn't know if that frightened him or excited him. All he knew was that Madison did both.

The urgency built. Hips fused together, they followed the music to the end until it faded and drifted away.

Exhausted, Madison fell back against her pillow. Duncan slowly lowered himself, careful not to hurt her, then seemed to melt against her body. She smiled, running her fingers over his hair. It felt damp. The thought filled her with immense satisfaction.

So, this was it. This was happiness. This was love. Very habit-forming. She turned her face into his hair, absorbing the scent, the feel. "I think I'm getting the hang of this."

Slowly, Duncan raised his head and looked at her. He felt half-dead and more alive than he could remember. "Getting it? Lady, if you were any better, it'd be illegal in at least forty-seven states."

A laugh bubbled in her throat. "Would you have to arrest me?"

He loved seeing the laughter in her eyes. It was so pure, so clean. Just like she was. She could make him forget, at least for a moment, that a darker, harsher world existed only a few feet away.

He nodded in reply. "Afraid so."

She didn't bother trying to keep a straight face. "Solitary confinement?"

Duncan pretended to think that over. As he did, he slowly began to stroke her. He could feel her shifting beneath him. It seemed humanly impossible, but she was arousing him again.

"Maybe not so solitary," he allowed.

Two could play this game. She ran her hand lightly along his back, down the slope of his spine and slowly along his buttocks. The expression on his face told her all she needed to know. "As long as I'm allowed one visitor."

Because he was leaning over her, the scar on his shoulder looked vivid now. She winced, thinking how much it must have hurt when he'd received the wound.

"So, are you going to tell me any more about how you got that?" she asked.

The world that he knew, the one where he had received the scar, was far too dirty for her to hear about. Duncan opened his mouth to tell her as much, then heard the tiny wail. He smiled, rolling off to one side. "Saved by the baby."

Madison dug her elbows into the mattress and propped herself up. There'd be other opportunities and she wouldn't let him squirm out of them. She meant to become part of his world, all of it. Only then would he begin to accept her.

"It's just a temporary reprieve." Getting up, she reached for her nightgown. She could feel his eyes on her as she slipped it on. Her body tingled in anticipation again. She lingered just a moment. "Will you be here when I get back?"

He pretended not to get her meaning and shrugged. "It's my house."

Laughing, she swiped at him playfully, hitting

Duncan's chest with the flat of her hand. "I mean, in my bed."

He caught her hand and held it, his eyes intent on hers. "That depends if you intend to carry on this Spanish Inquisition or not."

She knew he was only half teasing. He didn't like his privacy invaded. The world he worked in was off-limits. For now, she amended silently. Her expression was serious. "Not if it means you won't be here."

Duncan released her hand. She had to go to her son. He had no right to keep her, even if he felt like nipping along her body inch by torturous inch. "Then I'll be here."

He watched her leave the room, her hips swaying enticingly, issuing a silent promise. Was he crazy, feeling like this? Probably. But it was a moot point.

Taking a deep breath, he succeeded only in arousing himself. Her scent seemed to be everywhere, in her pillow, in the sheet, on him, and by inhaling deeply, he'd managed to fill his head with it.

Common sense dictated that he get up and go to his own room. The command was issued to deaf ears. Duncan folded his hands beneath his head and remained where he was. Just for tonight, he thought, common sense could take a flying leap.

Duncan slid from the bed as silently as he could, trying not to wake Madison. He was getting good at this, he mused, his lips curving. For the last eight days, they'd shared each other's beds, and he was getting very adept at rising without waking her.

What he wished he was equally adept at was not waking his feelings. Passion and desire were one thing—they were both normal. But it was the feelings of tenderness that worried him. He didn't want to have those kinds of feelings about her, and yet he didn't seem to have a say in the matter. They wouldn't be dictated to. They were just there, like tiny, vigilant glimmering lights.

He didn't have time to think about that now. He had to get going.

They'd made love twice last night, the second time at three in the morning after she'd put Neil down from his last feeding. Wild, passionate, almost frantic love. They had finally pushed each other beyond the scope of exhaustion. He'd been thoroughly convinced, in the last moments before he'd fallen asleep, that he would never be able to get up and move again.

The human body was more resilient than he'd previously believed, he thought with a smile. But Madison still needed to sleep. The baby would be demanding her attention again all too soon. It was best if she got what rest she could now. Duncan had several things to attend to before he went into the office today, but there was no reason to wake her.

No reason except that he wanted to kiss her again. To love her again. Make love with her again, he corrected himself, not love her. No matter what else he felt, he knew that part of him had been shut down for so long it could never be pried open again. The affection he held for Thomas was as close to loving as he could manage.

That wouldn't be enough for a woman like Madison.

But if he could have loved…it would have been her.

Maybe it was better this way, he thought as he gathered up his clothes, leaving her while she was asleep. If she was awake, he might not be able to make himself leave the room.

For a sliver of a second, he stood over Madison, looking at her. She was lying on her stomach, her cheek pressed against the pillow, her hair a wild blond sea about her face and shoulders.

With a touch that was light by necessity, he brushed away the hair obscuring her face. His heart swelled. It was a juvenile way for a grown man to act. He knew better. But it didn't seem to matter.

Madison's mouth dropped open. She sat up in bed, hugging her knees to her, trying to quell the stormy feeling in her stomach.

It was back.

All of it.

Every shred, every detail was back. Madison dragged her hand through her hair, stunned, trembling. She'd opened her eyes a few minutes ago to find Duncan had left. And her memory had returned. Without fanfare or preamble, without any warning. Boom, it just came back. No bump on the head, no startling revelations to jar her, nothing. It had returned like a thief slipping back to replace money taken from a church poor box.

She didn't know whether to laugh or cry. She did both.

Madison pressed her fingertips to her lips, keeping the sob back. Trying to gather her thoughts. She knew. She knew who she was. And what she'd been doing on that winding road when Duncan had run into her with his car.

Duncan. She had to tell Duncan.

Excitement telegraphed through her as she reached for the telephone, pulling it onto the bed. She'd punched in all but the last number of his cell phone when she suddenly stopped, her fingers freezing. A numbness descended over her. She let the receiver fall back into the cradle and replaced the telephone on the nightstand.

She didn't want to tell Duncan. Not over the telephone. And maybe not yet.

There was a dull throbbing in her head that was beginning to grow. Madison blocked it as best she could. She had to think.

If she told Duncan she knew who she was, she'd have to leave to reclaim her life. That meant leaving him. There'd be no reason for her to remain here any longer now that her memory had returned. And everything that might be between them would never have a chance to grow. She might love Duncan, but she knew he didn't love her. Not yet. If she left now, he never would.

Maybe it was horribly selfish, but she didn't want to give him up. Not when she'd finally found someone she loved.

Neil was stirring in the next room. Madison glanced at the clock. Four hours, right on the button. She swung her legs over the side of the bed and got up. If only she could count on everything else the way she could on Neil's cycle. Looking at the phone, she hesitated for a minute, debating. The receiver remained down. She hoped Duncan would forgive her for not telling him. But she just wanted a little more time with him before she broke the news.

* * *

The battle continued, fought over and over during the next few hours. Madison almost capitulated twice and actually called his cell phone once. When she heard his voice on the other end, her courage flagged.

"Hello?"

"Hi, it's me."

Duncan didn't have to be told who "me" was. He recognized her voice. Hell, he was certain he could even recognize her breathing pattern if put to the test. "Is anything wrong?"

"No." She damned herself as her waning courage disappeared completely. "I just wanted to hear the sound of your voice."

He tried not to let that mean anything to him. Told himself that it didn't. And yet he could feel a smile forming on his lips.

"You'll hear it loud and clear in a few hours." He looked around. There was no one close enough to hear. Duncan lowered his voice anyway. "What are you wearing? Right now, what are you wearing?"

"If I said applesauce, would you promise to lick it off?"

"The minute I get home." The word sprang up at him again. *Home*. Where the heart was. Where she was.

"When is that going to be?"

"I can probably get away by five. Six at the latest."

"Six," she repeated. Maybe she'd get her courage back by then.

"Hey, MacNeill, line two's for you. It's that detective you have going over the missing person's files. Kelly," Fontana called out to him.

Duncan signaled that he had heard and strode over to his desk. After almost a month, Duncan had thought Kelly had given up looking through the missing person's database. The man was a tenacious bulldog, he thought. He pushed down the first lit button in the row. "MacNeill here. Kelly?"

"Yeah. You sitting down?"

Adrenaline suddenly materialized, ready to spill. "Why, what did you find out?" Was she married after all? No, Kelly didn't know the situation between them. There was no reason for him to surmise that the relationship had become intimate. That wouldn't be why he'd asked if Duncan was sitting down. It had to be something else. "Tell me," Duncan demanded.

"One of the officers coming in from his shift saw this guy doin' seventy in a forty-mile zone. He pulls him over, the guy starts sweating, talking fast. They figure he's on something so they bring him in."

Duncan shifted. Kelly was not known for his short, terse answers. "Does this have a point, Kelly?"

"Yeah, and I'm getting to it. Turns out the guy matches a description of this guy who stuck up a convenience store not too far from where you live. They've got probable cause, so they search his car. Seems they find a purse in the trunk. There's even a wallet in it. The idiot didn't have enough sense to get rid of the driver's license in it. He claimed it belonged to his girlfriend, but he didn't know the name on it."

Digging for patience, Duncan asked, "Whose is it?"

"Well, at first they didn't know. They've got the name and everything, but the address isn't local. It's in Oakland. They think maybe it belongs to a mugging victim who was a tourist. So it's lying there on the desk, about to be taken and locked up, and I'm walking by. Being curious, I look.''

Duncan snapped the pencil in his hand. Fontana gave him a quizzical look, which he ignored. "The point, Kelly, the point.''

"Jeez, you take all the fun out of everything, MacNeill, you know that?''

"Yeah, I know that.'' Duncan couldn't shake off the growing feeling of dread, but he tried to ignore it. Just his natural pessimism taking over, that's all. "Who's the woman?''

"It's the woman you've been asking about. Her last name's Montclair.''

Madison Montclair. Had a nice ring to it, Duncan thought. He looked forward to saying it to her. "Great work, Kelly. I owe you one. I'll be down to pick up her purse as soon as I can.''

"Sure, no problem. I'll keep it for you until you can get here. Oh, one more thing. It's kind of a funny thing, too.''

Duncan couldn't explain why, but he felt a sharp prick of suspicion. "What is?''

"What she does for a living.''

It was like enduring a form of water torture. "What does she do?''

"She's a reporter. Her press card was in her wallet. I know how you feel about reporters. Just seems funny that you've had one in your house all this time without either of you knowing it.''

Duncan felt as if someone had just opened a trapdoor beneath his feet.

Fourteen

Darkness had swallowed the world by the time Duncan finally pointed his car toward the house. He'd stayed away as long as he could, trying to get a handle on his feelings. Trying to calm down. He hadn't been successful.

Anger, white-hot and searing, sizzled through his veins. Concentrating on the road was next to impossible.

How could he have been so stupid? He'd been a damn blind fool. Him. The one who examined everything and never took anything at face value. He'd taken her in and let his guard slip until it was almost down around his ankles.

Duncan cursed himself and her.

He'd allowed Madison to set him up and lead him around by the nose like some unsuspecting dupe. Worried that she might be a plant by the drug cartel, he'd missed the very obvious.

A reporter.

She was a reporter, for crying out loud. A damned, lousy, unprincipled, sneaky reporter. There was no doubt in his mind that she'd been out for a story, for a new angle. And, like a jerk, he had handed it to her on a silver platter.

He could even see the lead-in teaser: My wild

night with the country's most famous undercover man.

Damn you, Madison. Damn you for what you've done to me. Betrayal carved small, gaping holes in him. There were no words to describe the pain.

A truck, going too fast to stop, flew through the intersection. Duncan jammed on his brakes just in time. One more second and it would have been too late for either vehicle.

The forward momentum jarred him, reminding him of the accident he hadn't avoided. The "so-called" accident. He didn't doubt that was a setup, too. He was well acquainted with what an innovative reporter could do. Vacationing with his parents and traveling abroad, he'd seen reporters pose as hotel personnel, taxicab drivers and, once, as a nanny. His. All for another slant on the socialite who married the candy heir and their offspring.

He hit the steering wheel with the flat of his hand. The horn blared his outrage. It didn't help. Nothing helped.

Duncan glanced down at the speedometer. He was doing sixty. Uttering an oath, he eased his foot back from the accelerator. He didn't want to take his anger out on some unsuspecting bystander. He wanted to take it out on her. Not that it would do any good.

By the time he pulled up in his driveway, Duncan's fury had reached boiling point and was bordering on rage. He stood beside the car for a minute, trying to harness his temper. Right now, he wasn't sure what he was capable of. The thought of wringing her neck had definite pleasing aspects to it.

Damn it, she'd used him. Used his guilt and his

compassion against him until she'd tied him up in a knot. And if that wasn't enough, she'd beguiled him with those wide, innocent eyes of hers, with her enthusiasm mixed with shyness, her sweetness tangled with her subtle, unsettling sexuality.

Lies, all of it lies.

His stomach churned, knotted. She'd said she loved him the first night they spent together. She'd said the words so effortlessly, so sincerely he'd actually thought she meant it. And slowly, over the days, he'd allowed himself to believe that maybe... He had actually begun to wonder what it would be like if he was able to love her.

It had all been a sham. And he was the world's biggest fool because he'd bought into it. The whole nine yards. Like some naive, starry-eyed adolescent, he'd bought into it. He should have known better. But he hadn't.

Suddenly desperate for release, Duncan punched the driver's side of the car. He was too agitated to notice the sting in his knuckles.

Madison had long since stopped watching the program on the television set, though she kept it on for company. Where was he? It was almost nine and he'd told her that he would be home by five. She'd taken for granted that meant six. Seven at the latest. The grandfather clock in the hall had dragged the minute hand around for almost two full revolutions since seven and he still wasn't here, still hadn't called.

Madison tried not to worry, but the sight of his scar kept materializing in her mind. He'd acted as if

the scar were nothing. Commonplace. Which meant
that danger always rode shotgun beside him.

She looked accusingly at the telephone behind her.
Why hadn't he at least called to tell her he'd be late?

He wasn't calling because they weren't at that
stage yet, she told herself. He didn't owe her explanations. He didn't owe her anything. Just because
she'd given him her heart didn't bind him to her.
She'd given it to him freely. Without strings, remember?

It didn't help. Nerves began to knit scenarios in
her head. Horrible scenarios. Oh God, what if he
wasn't calling because he couldn't? Because something had happened to him?

The front door slammed shut and Madison
jumped, her heart thudding against her chest with the
force of a runaway truck. She suspected that something must have gone very wrong with the hearing
preparation. She turned on the sofa, rising partway
on her knees.

The next minute, he was in the room. The dark
scowl on his face told her she'd made the right assumption. Something had gone wrong. He looked almost unapproachable. She stayed where she was.
"Bad day?"

Duncan shoved his hands deep into his pockets to
keep from doing something he'd regret later, if not
now. He fisted them, digging his nails into his palms,
hard. She looked so damn innocent....

Hell, she looked virginal, too, and she wasn't that,
either. Illusions, all illusions. Just as he'd always
known. Until recently.

Just went to show what a fool he was.

"You might say that."

The way he growled his reply made Madison uneasy, although she couldn't pinpoint why. Remaining where she was, she tried to distract him by making simple conversation.

"Rosalie isn't here." She watched his face for a reaction. What she'd done had been presumptuous on her part. Madison hoped he'd take it the right way. "Angela was having a birthday party, so I told Rosalie to take the day off and come back tomorrow."

She was very good at manipulating the scene, wasn't she? Well, why not? Maybe her story needed a punchier ending. Maybe she even thought she could maneuver him into a proposal.

Duncan couldn't take the charade any longer. "Why? So you could seduce me without worrying about being interrupted? Maybe we can do it in the living room this time. Or I could sweep you off your feet and carry you up the stairs, like in *Gone with the Wind.*"

There was no smile on his face. He was biting off his words, firing them at her like bullets. Like accusations. Stunned, confused, Madison stared at him. "What?"

He was tired of waltzing around the truth. She was sitting there, all confused innocence, when she had lied to him. Over and over again. Was still lying to him. Bitterness rose in his throat, tasting like bile.

His voice was low, dangerous. "How long did you think you could go on pulling it off?"

She had never seen him like this. It took everything Madison had not to recoil. "Pull what off?"

"Pretending." He spit the word out.

Her heart stopped. How could he have known that

her memory had returned? It just wasn't possible. She hadn't breathed a word to anyone, not even Rosalie.

Had he read it in her face when he walked in? Embarrassed, Madison crossed to him and placed her hand on his arm. She was stunned and hurt when he jerked away. "I was just trying to buy a little time."

Something in him had wanted her to deny it. To make him believe that this was all a mistake. He figured that made him pathetic. "So you admit it."

She shrugged, helpless, not understanding why he was so angry with her. It wasn't as if she'd lied outright to him. She just hadn't called him when her memory returned. "I guess I have to, since you know."

"No clever explanations, no ruse?" His lips twitched in the semblance of a cynical smile. "I must say I'm disappointed." His eyes burned into hers as even that smile faded. "Damn disappointed."

"It just came back."

He stared at her as if she'd suddenly started babbling. "What came back?"

Madison had the feeling that she was trying to find her way in a field pockmarked with land mines. The phrases fell from her lips in staccato fashion. "My memory. This morning. Without any warning." She peered at his face. "Isn't that what you're talking about?"

How long was she going to try to keep this up? "Cut the theatrics, Madison. I know what you are, Madison Montclair."

He knew her last name. Why hadn't he said that from the beginning? She didn't understand what was going on, but she understood the look in his eyes.

Madison knew hate when she saw it, and it was assaulting her in waves.

Her chin shot up defensively. "What I am?" she repeated. "What do you mean, you know what I am? What am I?"

"A reporter." To him, that was worse than any curse he could utter. "A reporter who'd do damn near anything in her power to get her story." He circled her, as if trying to find her least offensive side. "I've got to hand it to you, you had me going there for a while. You really had me believing you had amnesia."

The implication of what he was saying seeped in and took her breath away. Wounded, she narrowed her eyes until they were hardened slits.

"Is that what you think? That I made this all up just to get a story?"

"Hey, take credit where credit is due," he said bitterly, his words mocking her. "This was very elaborate on your part. A regular three-act play. The pregnancy was a nice touch."

Fury rose in her chest, icy and fierce as it carved into her heart. She couldn't believe he was saying this to her.

"Did you like that?" Sarcasm dripped from her every word. "I thought it came off pretty well myself. It was digitally enhanced, you know, the pregnancy. And Neil is really animatronic."

She felt like throwing something, like screaming at him. It was all she could do to keep the tears back. She'd be damned if she let him see her cry. Frustrated, she started to take a swing at him, then dropped her hands to her sides. How could he? How *could* he?

''You big, dumb jerk!''

Now she was playing the wronged woman. With panache yet, but it was too late. Duncan saw through her. He was never going to forgive himself for being so blindly stupid. And he was never going to forgive her. ''Surely as a reporter you've got better words at your disposal than that.''

It was hopeless. He was going to believe what he wanted to believe. Condemn her without a hearing. Well, who needed him? Not her. She had her pride. Finally.

''Yes, I do, but I won't waste them on you.'' She turned and started out the door.

He caught her wrist and jerked her around to face him again. ''Where are you going?''

Glaring at him, she pulled her hand free. ''To get my son and get out of here.''

She had nerve, he thought, acting as if he'd wronged her instead of the other way around.

''Well, what am I supposed to think?'' he demanded, although for the life of him, he didn't know why he didn't let her just walk out. ''There's no missing person's report on you, there's nothing to indicate that you've disappeared. And then the police pull over some two-bit thief with your purse in his trunk.''

Her eyes widened in surprise. ''They found my purse?''

She wasn't even trying to deny it, was she? Why did that hurt? Was he that much of an idiot? ''Right along with your wallet and press card.''

He said it like an accusation. How could she have thought she was in love with him? He was a monster. A heartless monster.

"And naturally you jump to the conclusion that I planned all this. The accident, conveniently going into labor when you found me—"

"Labor can be induced," he countered.

She couldn't believe what she was hearing. The last shred of hope disappeared. "God, how do you manage to stand upright? With all that ego, I would think you'd be too top-heavy to walk." She hated him for what he was saying. "No wonder you're undercover. You're too loathsome to be out in public as yourself."

Neil's cry echoed above her raised voice. The sound cut into her anger, slicing it in half. It didn't matter about her. All that mattered was Neil.

She squared her shoulders, daring Duncan to try to stop her. "Now, if you'll excuse me, my animatronic son wants me." She crossed to the doorway. "Maybe it's not too late to have his name changed."

Duncan watched her walk out, his anger clawing at him. He desperately wanted to vent it. Almost as desperately as he wanted to call her back. But that was only physically motivated, he told himself. He couldn't forgive her for lying to him. For deceiving him.

Swearing under his breath, he went to pour himself a drink. The first of several.

Madison didn't want to cry, refused to cry. Because she knew that once she started, she wouldn't be able to stop. So she sat there in Neil's room, in the dark, feeding her child and rocking to comfort herself as much as him.

Her heart ached so much that she could barely draw a breath. She'd really believed that beneath

Duncan's stony exterior was a kind, gentle man. After the way he'd behaved these last few days, she thought she had proof.

Showed what she knew. Beneath the stony exterior was an even stonier interior.

She squeezed her eyes shut.

Damn him, anyway.

A tear slipped out between her lashes, trickling down her cheek. She brushed it away with the back of her hand, fighting for composure.

It would serve him right if she did write a story on him. Since she was a freelance writer, she could easily auction it to the highest bidder without any qualms of conscience.

But that was just the problem, she thought as she continued to rock, she had far too much of a conscience to do something as hateful as that. Even to him.

She pressed her lips together, trying very hard to keep a sob from escaping. It took her a moment.

"Certainly has been an education for us, hasn't it, Neil?" she whispered softly. "Count yourself lucky. From here on in, you're the only man I intend to trust. So don't cross me, okay?" Her voice cracked.

Neil gurgled his reply.

Madison sniffed. "Oh, now, there you go, arguing with me just like a typical man." She bit her lower lip as she fought back tears.

Madison lay awake all night, waiting for a knock on her door.

Waiting for an apology that didn't come.

She would have forgiven him if he'd apologized. Maybe that was weak of her, but she knew it was true. If Duncan would just say that he was sorry, that he wasn't himself when he had said those things and that he hadn't meant to hurt her, she would sweep it out of the way as if it hadn't happened. She would do that because, heaven help her, she still loved him.

But she could have spared herself the trouble of an internal debate. The knock never came.

At seven, she heard the front door slam. Duncan had left the house. Without talking to her.

Madison forced herself to get up. Her body felt as if it weighed a ton. Undoubtedly all those tears she hadn't shed, she thought.

She didn't know how much time she had. She wasn't sure if he'd left for the day or if he'd be back. Either way, she intended to be gone before he returned. There was no way she could remain here, not after the words that were said last night.

Words he hadn't even tried to take back. She damned him for that even more than for the words themselves.

"Face it, sweetheart," she murmured to Neil as she changed him. "Your mom's just not very smart about the men she falls in love with." A sad smile played on her lips. "No offense, honey."

She planned to leave everything Duncan had bought for her and for Neil. He could probably return most of the things and get his money back for them. Just to even matters, she intended to write him a check as soon as she could get her hands on her checkbook to cover any "mental pain and suffering" he might have endured because of their liaison. The bastard.

She hurried as fast as she could, not wanting to

stay a moment longer than she had to. She'd take her car. It was still in the garage.

She owed him for that, too, she thought ruefully. "The tab keeps mounting, doesn't it?" she muttered to Duncan, even though he wasn't there.

Dressed, Madison threw the barest essentials for Neil into a bag. Like a woman possessed, she was focused only on one goal. To get out of the house before she started to cry.

She never heard the back door open until it was too late.

Fontana gave up trying to concentrate on the data he'd pulled up on his monitor. It was impossible to ignore what was going on one desk from his.

He turned in his chair and looked at Duncan. He was surprised that Duncan's desk was still standing, given all the slamming and banging the man had subjected it to.

"Hey, what's with you? You've been acting like an angry bull in a china shop ever since you came in this morning."

Duncan stopped himself just short of hurling a binder across the room. Why wasn't anything where it was supposed to be?

"Just anxious to get this case wrapped up, that's all," he answered curtly.

The look Fontana gave Duncan said he didn't believe a word of it. "I'm anxious, too. You don't hear me snapping heads off, do you?"

Duncan slammed the middle drawer shut for the third time. Where the hell was that paper he was looking for? "We all have different ways of working." The phone on his desk jangled shrilly. Cursing, he jerked up the receiver. "MacNeill here."

"So, how is it going?"

He was in no mood to exchange pleasantries. The grand jury convened in less than three hours and there were still things he had to review. He had no time for unrelated phone calls.

"Who is this?" Duncan demanded.

"A pen pal." The voice on the other end paused. "Actually, I suppose that is not strictly true because that would mean you would have to answer my letters. And you do not know where to send them, do you?"

Duncan snapped to attention, catching Fontana's eye. Duncan silently signaled to the man to have the call traced. Fontana hurried to comply.

The chuckle in his ear sent an icy shiver up and down Duncan's spine.

"Do not bother having this call traced. I shall save you the trouble. I am calling from your house. Your very big, very grand house. I could almost believe you are a drug lord, it is so splendid. But do not worry, I will not be here long. I just came to get something." The laugh was sharp, cutting Duncan to the bone. "Actually, two somethings."

Duncan could feel his blood turn cold even as sweat began to trickle down between his shoulder blades. The vaguely familiar voice on the other end of the line was talking about Madison and Neil. When he spoke, Duncan's voice was as steely as the one in his ear was malevolently friendly. "What is it you want?"

"What I have always wanted, *amigo,* since I discovered your true colors. For you to find out how it

feels to have everything blow up in your face. Fig-
uratively speaking, of course.'' The voice laughed
softly and sounded all the more dangerous for it.
''You know, an eye for an eye, like in the Bible, eh,
amigo?''

Panic assaulted Duncan, striking at him from all
sides. He refused to let it come through in his voice.
It would sign Madison and Neil's death warrant and
he knew it. ''Don't hurt them. They have nothing to
do with this.''

The man on the other end had another opinion,
and his was the one that ultimately counted. ''Oh,
but they have everything to do with this. They are in
your house, in your life. Your very pathetic life.''
Hatred dripped from his every word. When he spoke
again, his voice was calm, suave. ''Tell me, they
mean a great deal to you, these two, do they not?''

Duncan didn't waste time with protests. If the man
on the other end of the line was who he thought—
Raul Montenegro—he wouldn't be convinced. He
only understood one thing. Brute force.

''You touch them and I'll kill you.'' Emotion be-
trayed him and throbbed in Duncan's voice. ''I swear
I'll hunt you down and kill you.''

It was a game to the other man, one in which he
enjoyed stacking the deck in his favor. ''Worth the
risk, my friend. Oh, and that policeman in the car
outside your house? I would notify his widow if I
were you. I guess it is the same everywhere, eh? You
just cannot get good help these days, can you?'' The
next moment, a dial tone buzzed in Duncan's ear.

Fontana stared at him. ''Who the hell was that?''

Duncan was already running toward the doorway.
He had to get to his house before it was too late.

"Tell Stringburne to send backup. Montenegro's turned up. He's killed Marquez and he's at my house right now."

"You're kidding me." But Fontana was talking to no one. Duncan was gone.

Fifteen

Madison's arms were beginning to ache. She held Neil close to her, afraid to put him down for even a second. She had no idea what the man standing in Duncan's living room was capable of. Standing only a little taller than her, he was rather an ordinary-looking man, the kind who wouldn't have made her look twice if she passed him on the street.

But there was nothing ordinary about the gun in his hand. And nothing friendly about the spine-numbing smile on his lips.

Neil began to whimper and she knew that he was hungry. Madison patted her son's back, trying to soothe him. She held on to her nerves as best she could. Neil couldn't afford to have her break down.

The man had made her stand less than a foot away, his gun trained on her as she told him Duncan's number at work. She'd listened to the call and realized that he wasn't just a common thief breaking in. He had a score to settle.

Was this what Duncan lived with all the time, the threat of death at any moment? How did he stand it? Madison tried to bank down her fear. It wouldn't help her. "What is it you want from me?"

His dark eyes seemed to stalk her as he slowly circled. She knew he was doing it to frighten her. But knowing didn't keep the fear at bay.

"Ah, I do not want anything from you. It is your lover I want. A pretty lady like you, I think he will be willing to trade his life for yours and his baby."

Boy, did he have the wrong number all around. She knew it was a long shot, but maybe the truth would send the man on his way. Madison raised her chin, her eyes as frosty as she could manage.

"If you mean Duncan MacNeill, this is not his baby and he is not my lover. And if you expect him to trade you anything for us, then you are in for a major disappointment."

For a split second, the man looked as if he were having second thoughts, but then contempt took over his features. "You expect me to believe that?"

Madison brazened it out, praying her voice wouldn't crack. She turned as the man continued to circle her, keeping her eyes on him at all times.

"You don't have to believe anything I say. You'll find out for yourself soon enough." She lifted one shoulder in a careless shrug, grateful she didn't tremble. "If he even bothers coming home."

His temper got the better of him, flashing in his eyes. Montenegro raised his gun until it pointed directly at her chest. Turning so that Neil was shielded by her body, Madison struggled not to step back.

"If you are not his woman, what are you doing living with him? You are far too damn sexy to be the housekeeper."

Madison stalled for time. She tried to think, clutching at fragments of the truth and trying to weave them into something that sounded plausible.

"I'm here because MacNeill ran his car into mine and sent me to the hospital. He feels guilty, but that's all. I don't mean anything to him." She ignored the

bitter sting the words carried with them. Saving Neil
was all that mattered now.

The man sneered, a sliver of doubt creeping into
his voice. "You are making this up to save him and
yourself. Even if he hit you with his car, why would
he bring you to his house?" he demanded angrily,
waving the gun as he spoke.

She was getting to him, she thought. Her eyes
trained on his weapon, Madison pushed further. "Because I don't have any place to stay. I lost my job
because of MacNeill's carelessness."

Her mind racing, she kept fabricating details as she
went along, praying she could think of something by
the time Duncan came. She knew Duncan would
come. His sense of honor would win out over any
lack of feelings he had for her. It was his job to
capture this man, even if it didn't matter to him
whether she and Neil were being held prisoner.

Her mouth felt dry as she continued. "MacNeill's
got a lot of money, so he can afford to pay to ease
his conscience."

Montenegro was not convinced. He was standing
close to her now, and his eyes glittered with hostility
that was barely suppressed.

"Why here?" he wanted to know. "Why not at
some hotel?"

Her mind seized the first word that came to her.
"Publicity." She quickly embellished her reply.
"MacNeill hates publicity and he's afraid that I'll
talk to the reporters, tell them he's a reckless driver,
that he almost killed the baby and me. Damaging
things like that."

It was the wrong thing to say. "Now I know you
are lying. He is getting a lot of publicity. I see the

broadcasts, read the newspapers. His face is everywhere, like a preening peacock."

Damn it, Madison, think. Think. You've got to do something before this crazy man starts shooting. "That's all positive. MacNeill hates negative publicity." She emphasized the word *negative*.

Madison was having a hard time keeping her mounting fear out of her voice. Desperate, she concentrated on the man's face, trying to read it, searching for any indication that he might be backing off.

He looked as if he were torn between calling her a liar and believing her. She could tell that he didn't want to believe her. The menacing expression completely contorted his face. His eyes slid from the baby in her arms to her face.

"Know what, pretty lady? I think you are lying. I think you are lying to save your worthless neck and the neck of that bastard of yours."

He sounded as if he were contemplating their execution. Fear squeezed her heart harder. Her voice came out in a whisper. "I thought you just wanted MacNeill."

He saw her fear and relished it. "MacNeill, you, the kid, it makes no difference to me." The smile on his lips froze the blood in her veins. "Three bullets are just as easy to fire as one, you know? After the first, it gets to be kind of fun." His eyes darted to his watch, then back to her. "Now, the way I see it, your lover should be here soon." He was proud of the work he had put into this. "I have seen this *hombre* drive when he is in a hurry, and he should not have a license." He laughed at his own words, then his expression turned threatening. He pointed the gun's muzzle at the sofa. "Please, sit down with your baby and we shall wait for him to rush to your rescue—and his untimely death.''

When Madison made no move to obey, the man drew back the hammer on his weapon, aiming it at Neil. ''I only ask once.''

Her heart in her throat, Madison sank down on the sofa. She wound her arms around Neil protectively. If there was only something she could do. ''Please, he's just a baby—''

Her words had less than no effect on Montenegro. He shrugged carelessly. ''Babies grow, become men. I was a baby myself once.''

It was impossible for her to picture him any other way than the way he was right now. A cold-blooded killer. ''Your mother must be very proud.'' The sarcasm came unintentionally.

His face was completely devoid of expression. ''My mother is dead. She died from an overdose of heroin when I was ten.'' The information was spoken without an iota of feeling.

''Then why are you involved in this?'' It was beyond Madison's comprehension.

He laughed again. ''Money, pretty lady, money. I am involved because of the money.'' Impatient, the man looked at his watch again. ''Where is he?''

Montenegro's back was to the doorway, but Madison was facing it. Her heart stopped completely as she saw Duncan slip in. He placed his finger to his lips, signaling her to give no indication that he was here. She looked up at Montenegro, determined to keep him talking until Duncan was close enough to get the drop on him.

''I told you he wouldn't come. He doesn't care about us.''

Anger rose, bringing a reddish hue to Montenegro's tanned complexion. "You had better pray that he does, and soon, or I will shoot you just to dirty up his fine white rug."

She saw Montenegro's eyes widen. Too late she realized that he saw Duncan's reflection in the window behind her. She tried to bolt, but in one swift movement, he jerked her to her feet. Swinging around to face Duncan, he kept her and the baby between them as a shield.

Duncan swore. His gun was aimed impotently over their heads. He couldn't get a clear shot. "Let them go," he ordered.

"Not on your life, MacNeill, or should I say St. James?" Montenegro's tone was mocking as he addressed Duncan by the name he'd used while undercover. "See, pretty lady, I told you he would be here for you." Using the tip of the muzzle, he stroked her cheek. He enjoyed the anger he saw igniting in Duncan's eyes. "You have excellent taste, my friend. Too bad you have no brains."

"Let them go, Montenegro," Duncan repeated. "I'll do what you want, just let them go."

"Duncan, no!" Madison cried, but Duncan ignored her.

"Very touching." Montenegro tightened his hold about her waist with a sudden jerk, almost squeezing the air out of her. "And you, my friend, will do what I want, all right. And what I want is for you to die. First you, then your bastard, then your woman." Montenegro's voice became low, like a predator about to spring. "After I am done with her, of course. Or perhaps I should let you live long enough to watch that, eh? It can be one final thing we share. You watching, me doing.''

Duncan played for time. He knew he'd beaten the other men in the department here, breaking all the speed limits. But they should be here soon. What he needed was to distract Montenegro for just a split second. Just one second and the man would be his.

But his thinking was clouded by the fear he saw in Madison's face. He had to save her. At all cost, he had to save her and the baby. His eyes locked with Montenegro's. ''You don't have to do this.''

''Oh, but I do.'' The words were slow, mocking. ''You have left me nothing else. The cartel is gone, the source is gone, I have nothing. Nothing but my honor. And my honor wants revenge. Now, who will it be? Who will go first? The bastard, you or your whore? Me, I think it'll be—''

He was so busy taunting Duncan, his attention had strayed away from Madison. Her heart hammered loudly, almost making her deaf. She couldn't just stand by and wait for something to happen. Any minute, he was going to kill Duncan.

It was now or never.

With her free hand, Madison jerked Montenegro's hand to her mouth and bit down on it hard. His gun went off, firing wild as he screamed obscenities at her.

''Duck!'' Duncan yelled at her. Madison tucked her head down, throwing her arm over the baby. Duncan fired at Montenegro almost at the same time.

Montenegro cursed Duncan's soul as he fell backward, away from Madison. Neil was howling. Madison felt her knees give way and buckle beneath her.

Duncan was there to catch her and Neil.

Struggling against blacking out, Madison pulled away from him.

"I'm all right, I'm all right," she cried hoarsely. "Just make sure he can't get up and hurt us."

Duncan needed only to glance where the bullet had struck Montenegro. True to his aim. There was no way the man was alive.

Duncan's voice was dispassionate. "He won't be hurting anyone anymore."

The next moment, there were DEA agents bursting in through the windows and doors, closing in like ants around an open jar of honey.

"Looks like we got here too late," one of the men commented, looking down at Montenegro's body.

"Try harder next time," Duncan said dryly. There was no sarcasm in the words. He'd almost been too late himself, he thought, then shut the realization away. He couldn't go there.

Questions were being fired at him. He fielded a few, then left the recording of the physical details to the others. He'd deal with all that later. Right now, he had only one thing on his mind—assuring himself that Madison and Neil had escaped with no ill effects.

One of the agents was holding Neil. Fontana had brought Madison a glass of water and was standing over her as she drank. Duncan nodded at him. "I'll take over from here."

Fontana held his hands before him in surrender. He knew when to back away.

Duncan crouched down beside Madison and searched her face. "Are you sure you're all right?"

Madison could only nod. Now that it was over, she felt as if she were going to fall to pieces. She clutched the glass between her hands like a good-luck talisman. Though she sat very still, she was trembling inside. Duncan had almost been killed right in front of her.

Duncan looked unconvinced about her condition. "I could get some smelling salts."

But as he rose, she caught his wrist. And found her voice.

"I said I'm fine." She bit her lip. "I didn't mean to snap like that." She took a deep breath, then released it. It helped. A little. "Thanks for saving Neil. And me."

He didn't want her gratitude. "Looks like we saved each other. If you hadn't bitten his hand, he would have shot me. Most likely killed me."

He said it with no feeling whatsoever. What was wrong with him? Didn't he care if he lived or died? "That's one hell of a crowd you hang around with, MacNeill." She was being snappish again but she didn't care. He was lucky she didn't hit him, she thought. Her nerves felt as if they'd been fed through a paper shredder.

"They're not much on manners," he conceded. He didn't blame her for yelling. He didn't blame her for anything anymore. He just blamed himself.

She rose and he was on his feet beside her, blocking her way. "Where are you going?"

There was no point in lingering or drawing this out. "I was leaving when your 'friend' broke in. If you don't need my statement or anything—" she glanced toward Fontana "—I'll just get Neil and be on my way."

"I don't need your statement." But when she moved to go around him, Duncan took her hand in his and held it. She looked at him quizzically. "I need you."

"For what?" There was suspicion in her eyes.

It wasn't easy, but he made himself say it. "For everything."

She wasn't buying into this, not again. There had to be something she was missing. "I don't understand."

Not wanting an audience, he drew her aside, out of the way. Behind him, one of the agents was outlining Montenegro's body, another was taking photographs. Privacy was at a premium. "When I thought he was going to hurt you and Neil, something snapped inside of me."

She refused to be a fool twice. Once was more than enough. "That was probably just the lid on your secret identity snapping up. You're a superhero. You save people, remember?"

Her voice was cold and he knew he deserved that. Duncan placed his hands on her shoulders, his eyes on hers. "This time, it was different."

Her eyes narrowed as she shrugged him off. "Why? Because this time you had to go against everything you believed in and save a reporter?"

He deserved that, too, but it wasn't easy standing still for it. "You're making it hard, aren't you?"

She wanted to shout at him, to tell him how much he'd hurt her. Instead, she did her best to keep her voice low. "I thought I was making it easy on both of us. I was going to be gone before you got back, but he spoiled my getaway." She nodded toward Montenegro's body, refusing to look in that direction.

"So I guess, in a way, I owe him."

Was he deliberately playing with her mind? "You've lost me."

The casual phrase shimmered before him like a prophecy. "God, I hope not."

She could only stare at him uncomprehendingly. "Duncan, I think I still have some side effects left over from the accident. What are you saying to me?"

He was hoping he wouldn't have to spell it out. But so be it. He was going to do whatever it took to make her stay.

He took both her hands in his. "That I don't want you to leave. That I want you in my life. That for the first time since I can remember, I feel like smiling when I wake up." And it was all because of her. "I don't want to give that up."

"You weren't smiling this morning." It was a guess on her part, since she hadn't seen him, but she figured it was a sure thing.

"This morning I was an idiot."

"No argument." Still, she was slow to believe him this time. His words had been harsh. "What about all the accusations?"

It took a great deal to swallow his pride, but he would do it for her. "I overreacted."

"Damn straight you overreacted." She couldn't help the flash of temper that came.

He had to make her understand. He wasn't going to lose her. "But look at my background. I've been hounded by the press for one reason or another most of my life. All I wanted was to be left alone. My line of work gave me that. And then, suddenly, by doing exactly what I was supposed to do, everything blew up in my face. The microphones and the cameras were back.

"And then you came along and managed to seep through all the barriers in an incredibly short amount of time. When I found out you were a reporter, it was like someone had taken a knife and cut my heart out. I was sure you'd played me for a fool just to get a story."

Madison drew herself up, remembering the fear that had been with her just a few minutes earlier. Fear for his life. No matter what, she still loved him. "And now?"

"And now I don't care if you were or not. When I saw Montenegro point that gun at your head, everything froze inside. I thought he was going to kill you. I can't face that again—living in a world without you in it," he explained.

The sincerity in his eyes made her want to cry. "Everything inside of me says that I should tell you that's not good enough, that you should have believed in me...."

He heard the word even though she hadn't said it. "But?"

She blew out a breath. "But I never was a very good listener when it came to lectures. Even if I'm the one doing the lecturing."

Slowly, the fear slipped away. He wasn't going to lose her. "I was counting on that."

So much for playing hard to get, she thought. She never could indulge in games when it came to her heart. Madison pressed her lips together. "So where do we go from here?"

Ignoring the other people in the room, he slipped his arms around her waist. "I was thinking of a chapel or a justice of the peace, something along those lines."

Her mouth fell open. This was totally out of character. "Don't you want to know about me?"

Duncan shook his head. "Only if you want to tell me. Right now, I know all I need to know about you. That you're alive and that you're here."

Nice try, she thought. Her mouth curved. She already knew him too well to believe he'd be satisfied with just that. "You had me checked out, didn't you?"

He laughed. He liked a woman who was sharp. "Just enough to know you're not married and that Neil's father took off as soon as you told him you were pregnant." He'd checked that out as soon as he'd come in to the office this morning. That much he'd had to know—whether she'd lied to him about everything and was actually married.

She wanted him to know everything. They couldn't begin a life together under the shadow of uncertainty. "Neil's father was married. A little detail that never worked its way into our conversation until after I said I was pregnant." The devastation she'd felt at the time seemed a million miles away now. "He was somebody I worked with. I tried not to let it get in my way, but it did, so I finally quit my job and decided to relocate."

It all made sense now. "That was why there was no missing person's report on you."

Madison nodded. "I've no family to speak of and I was in transit." She remembered the events of the night of the accident vividly. "I was on my way to Newport Beach when I stopped at a convenience store. Unfortunately, so did the guy who held it up." She kept the memory at bay. "He wanted to use me as a hostage, but I managed to get away and to my car. I had my car keys in my pocket and I drove away as fast as I could." The robber was the man in her nightmares, she realized now. His was the face of the man she saw pursuing her. "I didn't stop until I started getting labor pains. I guess being traumatized had brought them on. I had to pull over. That was when you hit the car."

"And the jackpot."

He believed that, she realized. The thought warmed her. "I've only got one question for you."

He cocked his head. "As a reporter?"

"As anything." She studied his face, searching for his answer even as she asked, "Do you love me?"

Didn't she realize that by now? "Yes, damn it. That's the whole problem."

"Love is never a problem, Duncan. Only doing without it is." And then she smiled. "And you're never going to do without it again."

Fontana looked at his watch. Their safety margin was down to almost nothing. Though he hated to interrupt Duncan, he had to.

"Hey, MacNeill," he called to him. Duncan didn't even bother looking in his direction. "We've still got a grand jury to get to."

"Tell them to wait." He smiled down at Madison. "I've got something more important to do first."

"Like what?" Fontana wanted to know.

Duncan grinned, still looking at Madison. "Mind if I show him?"

Her mouth curved. "Be my guest."

He framed her face with his hands. "That's what I love, an accommodating woman."

Her smile began in her eyes, spreading swiftly until it took in all of her. All of him, as well. "Don't get too used to it, MacNeill. I plan to keep you on your toes.''

And she would, too. Anticipation filled him. ''Good, because I plan to enjoy being there.''

And then, because he couldn't resist any longer, Duncan kissed her. And realized that for his thirty-second birthday tomorrow, he was going to be exactly where he wanted to be. In Madison's arms.

* * * * *

Here's a preview of next month's

—————World's Most—————
Eligible Bachelors

Harrison Lawless
the hard-edged corporate tycoon from

HIS BUSINESS, HER BABY
by
Dixie Browning

Harrison Lancaster Lawless, founder, chief stockholder and, until recently, CEO of Lawless Inc., had been called a lot of things, including arrogant, stubborn and hard-nosed. He'd been called a bloody-minded, coldhearted pirate as well as a domineering control freak.

The one thing he had never been called was stupid. So, if he had to move out of the fast lane, after having led the pack for years, he would do it.

But he'd damned well do it his way.

And this, he thought, surveying the sprawling log house, was the way he intended to do it. In style, with comfort and privacy. Once he was settled in he could have a few pieces of equipment shipped down, take his time setting them up, and before long, he'd have another company up and running.

Single-handed. In less than a year.

He might have missed the house completely, so well did it blend in with its surroundings. But two things had caught his attention. A blue-and-white For Sale sign and a yellow-print nightgown flapping on a clothesline. A *big* nightgown, more in the style of Pillsbury Mills than Victoria's Secret.

He climbed the wooden stairs and knocked. The door swung open. "What do you want?"

God, she was a mess. Piles of straw-colored hair,

half of it pinned up on top of her head, half spilling down over her shoulders. Clear brown eyes. Too clear. And a damned sight too revealing. He summed up the parts and came up with the total.

Proud, determined and...vulnerable?

Vulnerable.

Oh, hell.

"I saw the sign. I believe I'll take it," he said.

"The sign?" Cleo blinked.

"The For Sale sign."

"You want my For Sale sign?"

He looked at her as if she were not quite bright. "I want your house," he said patiently.

"Look, whoever you are, I don't—" she began, but he was too busy gazing up at the vaulted ceiling, at the moose head, the bear head, the coatrack made of antlers.

"This is it," he said softly, almost reverently.

"No, it isn't." She crossed her arms, resting them on her protruding shelf of a stomach.

"It's already sold?"

"Well, no, not exactly."

"Are you the owner? It's still for sale, then?"

"Yes, I am, and no, it's not. I've changed my mind. This isn't a good time. For me, I mean. I'm uh—I'm expecting a baby."

"I noticed," he said dryly.

She detected a slight thaw in those granite gray eyes. In an ordinary man it might even have passed for amusement. But he was no ordinary man. "I'm sorry for your trouble. Driving all the way out here, I mean. Did the real estate agent send you? I'm sure she'll be able to find you something else."

"But you see, I don't want something else," he

explained gently, almost as if he were speaking to a child. "I want this place."

Harrison watched the words register and gauged their effect. She stared at him helplessly, her arms unconsciously cradling her bulging middle. She was a mess, he told himself. A genuine flake. Or maybe all pregnant women were this way. Never having been around one before, he couldn't say. "How much are you asking?" he said.

She named a figure. It was half what he'd expected. Either the lady was loco or property values down here were at rock bottom. "Sold," he said, his voice devoid of the jubilation he was feeling.

"No, it's not sold," she snapped. "I told you I've changed my mind. Look, I need to sit down. When I stand too long, all the iced tea I had for lunch runs down to my feet and ankles, and I can't get my shoes on."

Without waiting for a response, she plopped down onto the sofa.

"Do you need to consult your husband first?"

"I don't have a husband."

He looked pointedly at her third finger, left hand. Following his gaze, she covered her bare fingers with her other hand.

"My fingers are too swollen to wear my rings, and anyway, it's none of your business whether or not I'm married."

"You're right. All the same, the place was obviously built and furnished by a man. I just assumed—"

"Well, don't."

He lifted both his hands in a gesture of surrender. He watched her struggle to get up from the sofa, knew the exact moment when she surrendered to the inevitable. Her eyelids were shadowed. She looked tired. Tired and defeated, and vulnerable.

That word again. It made him feel uncomfortable. The women in his life were, without exception, about as vulnerable as sharks. He preferred strong, challenging women.

With his long-fingered hands bracing narrow hips, he reminded her of a pirate ruling from his poop deck, or wherever it was pirates ruled their ships from.

"You're not going to leave, are you?". She experienced a sinking feeling.

Neither of them said a word about the lodge. About the contract she'd signed with the real estate people and whether or not he could force her to honor it. Her stomach churned.

Well…shoot.

He just smiled. Standing there in his expensive shoes, with his thumbs hooked into the hip pockets of his expensive pants, he smiled again.

And she lay there in her mail-order tent dress, with her bare, swollen feet propped on a red-and-white cowhide pillow, and burst into tears.

Silhouette

SPECIAL EDITION™

SPECIAL EDITION

Stories of love and life, these powerful novels are tales that you can identify with—romances with "something special" added in!

Fall in love with the stories of authors such as **Nora Roberts, Diana Palmer, Ginna Gray** and many more of your special favorites—as well as wonderful new voices!

Special Edition brings you entertainment for the heart!

SSE-GEN

SILHOUETTE® Desire®

Do you want...

Dangerously handsome heroes

Evocative, everlasting love stories

Sizzling and tantalizing sensuality

Incredibly sexy miniseries like **MAN OF THE MONTH**

Red-hot romance

Enticing entertainment that can't be beat!

You'll find all of this, and much *more* each and every month in **SILHOUETTE DESIRE**. Don't miss these unforgettable love stories by some of romance's hottest authors. Silhouette Desire—where your fantasies will always come true....

DES-GEN

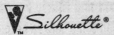

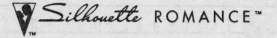

Silhouette ROMANCE™

What's a single dad to do when he needs a wife by next Thursday?

Who's a confirmed bachelor to call when he finds a baby on his doorstep?

How does a plain Jane in love with her gorgeous boss get him to notice her?

From classic love stories to romantic comedies to emotional heart tuggers, **Silhouette Romance** offers six irresistible novels every month by some of your favorite authors! Such as…beloved bestsellers **Diana Palmer, Annette Broadrick, Suzanne Carey, Elizabeth August** and **Marie Ferrarella,** to name just a few—and some sure to become favorites!

Fabulous Fathers…Bundles of Joy…Miniseries… Months of blushing brides and convenient weddings… Holiday celebrations… You'll find all this and much more in **Silhouette Romance**—always emotional, always enjoyable, always about love!

WAYS TO *UNEXPECTEDLY* MEET MR. RIGHT:

♡ Go out with the sexy-sounding stranger your daughter secretly set you up with through a personal ad.

♡ RSVP yes to a wedding invitation—soon it might be your turn to say "I do!"

♡ Receive a marriage proposal by mail— from a man you've never met....

These are just a few of the unexpected ways that written communication leads to love in Silhouette Yours Truly.

Each month, look for two fast-paced, fun and flirtatious Yours Truly novels (with entertaining treats and sneak previews in the back pages) by some of your favorite authors—and some who are sure to become favorites.

YOURS TRULY™:
Love—when you least expect it!

FIVE UNIQUE SERIES
FOR EVERY WOMAN YOU ARE...

❤ *Silhouette* ROMANCE™

From classic love stories to romantic comedies to emotional heart tuggers, Silhouette Romance is sometimes sweet, sometimes sassy—and always enjoyable! Romance—the way you always knew it could be.

SILHOUETTE® *Desire*®

Red-hot is what we've got! Sparkling, scintillating, *sensuous* love stories. Once you pick up one you won't be able to put it down...only in Silhouette Desire.

Silhouette®SPECIAL EDITION®

Stories of love and life, these powerful novels are tales that you can identify with—romances with "something special" added in! Silhouette Special Edition is entertainment for the heart.

SILHOUETTE·INTIMATE·MOMENTS®

Enter a world where passions run hot and excitement is always high. Dramatic, larger than life and always compelling—Silhouette Intimate Moments provides captivating romance to cherish forever.

❤ SILHOUETTE YOURS TRULY™

A personal ad, a "Dear John" letter, a wedding invitation... Just a few of the ways that written communication unexpectedly leads Miss Unmarried to Mr. "I Do" in Yours Truly novels...in the most fun, fast-paced and flirtatious style!